# NATURE'S GUARDIAN ANGEL

## John Muir

WAYNE HUNT

Inquiries and Book Orders should be addressed to:

Great Writers Media
Email: info@greatwritersmedia.com
Phone: (302) 918-5570

ISBN: 978-1-960939-29-6 (sc)
ISBN: 978-1-960939-30-2 (ebk)

# CHAPTER 1

## Natura's Assignment

*"For He will give angels charge over you to accompany, defend, and preserve you in all your ways. They shall bear you up on their hands, lest you dash your foot against a stone." Psalm 91:11-12*

"As you sit there reading this, whether you believe it or not, there is an angel by your side; it is your guardian angel, and it never leaves you. Each one of us has been given a gift, a shield made from the energy of light. It is a part of the guardian angel's task to put this shield around us. To God and the angels we are all equal; we all deserve to be protected, to be cared for and to be loved, regardless of what others think of us, good or bad." Lorna Byrne (1)

All the stars across the universe shined brightly, the planets revealed their purest colors as they gleefully reflected the Sun's super-hot, flaming rays; the glorious comets streaked across the giant cosmos going to places unknown, unseen; and the guardian angels sat in Heaven on a soft cloud outside the Great Decision Hall awaiting patiently, but excitedly, for their humankind assignments. Inside the great hall, the Archangels would soon meet with God to hear His announcement of the new guardian angels' assignments. Once every year, on January 1, God announced His decisions about which guardian angel would be assigned to which unborn human soul. It was one of the most glorious times in the

Kingdom of Heaven! Every Archangel, all the Saints, the angels who'd just graduated from the Guardian Angel University, and the host of all angels in Heaven gathered and prayed endlessly, "Holy, Holy, Holy, Lord God Almighty, Heaven and earth are filled with Your endless love and glory; praise to You, Heavenly Father, forever and ever".

In the midst of this great joy, the newly graduated guardian angels awaited God's announcement! They hardly said a word to each other, only beaming a few whispered thoughts as their hearts seemed to communicate through their loving, glowing eyes the many thoughts swirling within them.

"Natura", asked his best friend, Harry, "what humankind assignment do you want to receive?"

"I know we're not to wish about our assignments, nor even to think about the possibilities, but you know how much I've studied the wonders of the natural things God created on earth," Natura replied. "I don't know everything about the earth's creatures, plants, trees, mountains, and streams, but I know in my heart that one day I will. I also know that I'm ready to guide the human soul who receives the task of helping to conserve and protect these sacred natural resources."

As he finished beaming this message to Harry, his eyes seemed to glow more brilliantly than all the other angels.

"Yes, Natura, I understand what you mean. It is very difficult to say 'God's will be done' when our hearts yearn so much for an assignment that we know will truly make us happy. However, we surely trust that God knows what'll make us happy."

The rumblings of heavenly thunder boomed loudly inside the great hall. The guardian angels knew that God would soon enter the hall. He would take His seat on the high throne overlooking the grand gathering of archangels and many saintly guests.

Through the one large window of the great hall could be seen the planet Earth which God especially created for His personal love and enjoyment. No other planet in the universe had such rich land, an abundance of natural things, thousands of living creatures, and the only living creature made in His image. Man, humankind, God made in His very own likeness, gave him an eternal soul, breathed in him life, and sent him on a mission to love one another and to care for the earth's natural things.

As the archangels and the saintly guests rejoicingly bowed down, a cloud of bright, sparkling white light slowly shined in all directions to illuminate the hall and the entire universe beyond. The living presence of pure love, beyond measure and understanding, pulsed from the cloud's center, filling everyone and everything with an unspeakable peace and endless joy. No one image could be seen within the cloud; the great light was too brilliant to reveal anything but God's Holy Presence. His Presence did not speak but merely sent waves of living, loving words that were understood by all who heard them. While God's announcement lasted only a few minutes, the guardian angels' assignments were revealed for all graduating guardian angels. Instantly, everyone present could hear God's Living Words and clearly know His assignment decisions.

"Congratulations, Natura!" Harry said excitedly.

In a daze, shaking his head with disbelief, Natura's spiritual heart seemed to rapidly pound within his angelic body form. Harry's voice slowly weaved its way through Natura's subconscious mind so he could hear.

"Oh, yes, thank you Harry! I can't believe my deepest desire has come true! 'Nature's Guardian Angel' has been assigned to me!"

Natura turned toward Harry. "What assignment did you get, Harry? I was so caught up in God's thundering announcement that I didn't hear your assignment."

"I was assigned as 'a mighty spiritual warrior'!" Harry's whole body glowed with brilliant pulses of bright celestial light. "I will become part of God's mighty army of angels in their continuing battle to defeat Satan and his evil spirits. In my heart, I've dreamed of fighting Satan's evil army. That is why I was born and given the name, Harry, which means 'mighty in war'."

"I'm so happy for you, Harry!" Natura patted his best angelic friend on his back.

Both Natura and Harry raised their long wings, fluttered them with a whirring roar, and quickly soared to join the other guardian angels who were joyfully flying around the nearest stars in celebration of their assignments.

Suddenly the huge double doors of the great hall opened; thousands of trumpets sounded at once. The archangels paraded out of the doors through the most glorious fireworks of rainbow colors. Each of them would soon gather with their guardian angels to give them their first instructions. One by one, the archangels flew to meet with their guardian angels. Natura waited patiently for his archangel to arrive, whatever his name and whatever he looked like. He looked around, scanning the nearby universe for any signs of an archangel coming in his direction, but saw none. Time seemed to stand still. It seemed like an eternity to Natura.

"*Why am I alone*?" Natura thought. No sooner had he completed this thought than he was overshadowed with huge flapping wings that seemed to block out most of the universe's light.

"Natura, Natura, Natura!" a booming voice came from a giant angel who now stood face to face with him.

"Yes, sir, that would be me!" Natura nervously answered, afraid to look directly into the giant angel's blazing, fiery eyes.

"You, my dear angel, are assigned to me. My name is Archangel Raziel. I am the archangel responsible for caring for the natural things on earth, except, of course, for humankind. Well almost. There is one humankind, or human soul I should say, that I'm responsible for protecting and guiding. That's why I need your help, Natura."

"Yes, sir!" Natura waited for further instructions from Archangel Raziel.

"A special spiritual soul will be given to a Scottish boy to be named John Muir, who will be born in Dunbar, Scotland, on April 21, 1838. This boy will grow up to become one of the world's greatest naturalists who'll inspire others to love and preserve nature. His voice and his writings will be responsible for creating many national parks and forests in America. He will also be a great influence in encouraging Americans to care for these natural lands. You, Natura, will be responsible for protecting and guiding John Muir to become that special person. I, of course, will instruct you in how to do that. All the other angels in Heaven will also help you whenever you ask them. Are you ready to begin, Natura?"

"Yes, sir, I am ready!"

"Then let's be on our way to Dunbar, Scotland, where your training will begin. You'll have three months to learn your way around Dunbar, the Scottish language, the Scottish history, and all things natural. You'll also have to become acquainted with John Muir's family, that is, his parents, siblings, and grandparents."

Natura thought about all that he'd have to learn in three short months. He was both excited and a little nervous. He watched as Archangel Raziel warmed up his large wings with a few short flaps. "Whish!" the sound of Raziel's wings quickly took flight. Natura promptly followed. The two angels soared high over, under, and around the stars while navigating their way through streams of comets. Their destination was planet Earth and its little Scottish town of Dunbar.

# CHAPTER 2

## Natura's Training in Dunbar

*"When we contemplate the whole globe as one great dewdrop, striped and dotted with continents and islands, flying through space with other stars all singing and shining together as one, the whole universe appears as an infinite storm of beauty."* John Muir (2)

Moving at the speed of light, Raziel and Natura quickly entered the Earth's frigid atmosphere over the North Pole. They navigated southward to the great North Sea which separates Scotland and the rest of Great Britain from mainland Europe. Now flying low, and slower, they saw Scotland's beautiful Shetland Islands, located several hundred miles northeast of its mainland. Raziel and Natura were flying so low that they could see some of the island's Shetland ponies running playfully around lush green pastures. Soon, they flew over the Shetland Islands, and then over the Orkney Islands, another group of islands located just off Scotland's northeast coast. Both of these island groupings were populated by Scandinavian people in its early history and became a part of Scotland in the 15$^{th}$ century. Scotland also has many other islands, mostly located to the west of the mainland, in the Atlantic Ocean, just northeast of Ireland. Following Scotland's eastern seashore along the North Sea, Raziel and Natura flew southward, over Scotland's mountains, often called the 'Highlands', then over its hill country, and finally over its lowlands. Crossing the Firth of

Forth, a large sea inlet, they saw the little town of Dunbar, now overshadowed with a light, misty fog.

As they broke through the light fog covering the little town and approached its waterfront, they spotted an old, rundown castle, resting high on a cliff overlooking the great North Sea. They had already learned that the old red stone building and it protective walls were the remains of Dunbar Castle. Built in the 8th century by German people known as the Picts, the castle was almost impossible to penetrate during the many battles of its active life. It also has withstood many battles between Scotland and England over several centuries. However, the old castle has not been able to withstand the advances of the fierce North Sea waves. Slowly, over hundreds of years, these waves have washed through the castle's protective walls, heavily damaging its foundation. The sea's natural forces have slowly destroyed what massive human armies could not penetrate.

Next to the castle, two small protective harbors, Victoria and Cromwell, shelter the town's fishing boats from the turbulent North Sea waters. Raziel and Natura observed a crowd of fishermen busily unloading their day's catch of fish to sell to the waiting townspeople. Invisible to the townspeople, the two flew over them and fluttered to a soft landing on High Street at the home of Daniel and Anne Muir, soon to be the proud parents of a special boy to be named John Muir.

"Here we are, my boy, our home away from home," Raziel said to Natura.

Still invisible, even to each other, Natura clearly heard Raziel's words and saw a faint outline of his huge wings as they quietly came to rest.

"Yes, sir!"

"We'll go directly to an unoccupied room on the second floor so as not to disturb anyone," Raziel said.

The large, three-story stone house formerly belonged to a Dunbar physician before Daniel Muir bought it. The ghost of the old doctor is believed by many Dunbar citizens to reside in this dark, unoccupied room. Strewed around the room could be seen a variety of medical laboratory items left behind by the old doctor. Some Dunbar citizens even think he still uses the dusty glass tubing, flasks, and dishes for mixing chemical compounds to fill his ghostly-patients' prescriptions.

Raziel and Natura looked around the cluttered, dusty room and quickly made themselves comfortable. They have no luggage to unpack because, as angels, they have no need for clothing, pajamas, toothbrushes, soap, deodorant, towels, or anything else humans use. Raziel does have a large backpack-looking bag filled with books he'll use for teaching Natura.

Raziel slowly unloaded the bag containing street maps of Dunbar, history books about Dunbar and Scotland, Scottish language textbooks, nature books, and evil spirit battle books. These last books will become the most important because Natura will soon meet Satan and his devilish spirits. You see, all new guardian angels must first be tested by Satan before they're allowed to officially do their assigned work. Natura could clearly see the many books and their titles as Raziel organized them on a long laboratory work bench. His heart raced as he saw the battle books and considered the great spiritual battle he must fight. It would come sooner than he realized!

"Now with that done, Natura, let me present you with your training schedule for the next three months."

Raziel handed Natura a copy of several papers on which was written the name of the training, books to read, daily assignments, and examination dates. Natura looked surprised as his glowing eyes focused on the evil spirit battle training. It was at the top of the list! For some reason, Natura thought it would be further down the schedule. At least he hoped it would be because the encounter with Satan would be the most difficult thing he'd ever have to do in his angelic lifetime.

"I'll explain the training schedule to you. I can tell by the surprised look on your face that you see that 'battling Satan and his evil spirits' is at the top of the list."

"Yes, sir. I guess I thought it'd be further into the training schedule."

"I understand, Natura." Raziel looked a bit sympathetic but showed a posture of strength and toughness as his brilliant, blazing eyes focused squarely on Natura's eyes.

"But you must understand that this is the most important training of all. You cannot be a good guardian angel until you learn to reject Satan and all of his evil promises. Satan is very, very smart, but not smarter than God and his angels. Always remember that, Natura! Satan knows us angels very well and will try everything in his devilish book of tricks to convince us to worship him instead of our own loving God."

Raziel then handed Natura a book about how to win battles with evil spirits. Natura took the book, opened it to the first chapter, and began to silently read.

"Your assignment for tonight is to read the first chapter and to write a short essay about why you're smarter than Satan. We'll begin our class in the morning at six o'clock sharp! Try to get a good night's sleep because tomorrow will be a long, tiring day."

"Yes, sir! And a good night to you Archangel Raziel."

"Good night!" His blazing eyes quickly disappeared. Natura then saw Raziel's giant, ghostly shadow slowly stretch and gently levitate. That's how angels sleep. They don't need a bed like humans do.

Natura spotted an old desk across the room. He floated over to it, placed his textbook and writing notebook on it, and suspended himself in front of it to begin his first assignment. It had already been a long day because he and Raziel had traveled millions of miles from Heaven to Earth. Although he was tired, he was also very excited, and a little apprehensive to learn about battling evil spirits. He imagined that his best friend, Guardian Angel Harry, must also be studying about evil spirits as he prepared to become a spiritual warrior in God's army of angelic warriors.

Around midnight, Natura finished reading the first chapter and with his special writing pen, wrote at the top of the first page in his notebook, 'Why I Am Smarter than Satan'.

"Why am I smarter than Satan? Why am I smarter than Satan?" he repeated aloud to himself, nervously tapped his angelic pen on the desk, and looked around the dark room as if he'd find an answer somehow. Remembering what he'd just read in the first chapter, and thinking about it, he wrote.

> *"I am smarter than Satan because I'm made in God's image and His Spirit is in me. He loves me with a very deep and endless love. He will never leave me alone or forsake me. Even though I'll experience trials in my life, He'll always be beside me to tell me what to do and what to say. So, I don't ever have to be afraid of anything or anyone, especially Satan. I know that Satan is very smart and that he will try many things to turn me against God. He'll try to convince me that I can do everything myself and that I'll be better off in my life without God. I know this is not true. And as one of God's guardian angels, I am made to be one of His special messengers and have been assigned to protect and guide John Muir through his earthly life. I'm very happy about that! I know that as long as I obey God, trust Him, and ask Him for His help in everything, He'll always make me smarter than Satan."*

"There, that should do it." Natura said out loud to himself.

Unknown to him, Raziel was still awake and heard Natura read his short essay out loud. Raziel smiled to himself and thought that Natura had done a very good job on his first assignment. He closed his eyes and went to sleep. Natura also went to sleep. Well, at least he tried to sleep.

Feeling somewhat satisfied with completing his first assignment, and also feeling very tired from a very long trip, Natura quickly went to sleep. After a few hours of sound sleep, seven evil spirits entered Natura's dream space and pretended to be his own dreaming conscious. In rather loud dream voices, the evil spirits said, "I am not going to be a good guardian angel because I know I can't succeed in the examination event with Satan. He's too powerful for me. I should just give up now, return to Heaven, and become an ordinary angel." "No, I can't do that!" Natura's own dream conscious said. "God would not have chosen me to be a guardian angel if He thought I couldn't do it well." "Sometimes God makes mistakes!" One of the seven evil spirits said. "He probably did with me. I'm just going to be a failure."

Back and forth went the conversation in Natura's dream space. He struggled to maintain some sense of mind control but he couldn't. He even tried to return to his full consciousness but he couldn't. His angelic body began to twist and jerk. Raziel was awakened by Natura's restless movement. He saw a dark shadow surrounding Natura's head and immediately knew that evil spirits had entered Natura and were trying to possess him. Raziel knows that Natura's spiritual body is weak because he has not been fully trained and is still very inexperienced. And he knows exactly what to do!

Raziel hovers close to Natura and wills his own spirit to enter Natura's dream space where it joins with Natura's spirit. Together their two spirits form a shield around Natura's soul which safely encloses it. The seven evil spirits become agitated and confused. They no longer are able to converse with Natura's dream conscious. Slowly they see that they're on the outside looking in and can't reside in his space any longer. As they look closer at Natura's spirit, they see another spirit, a much stronger spirit joined with his spirit which makes it impossible for them to penetrate. Realizing they've lost this battle to possess Natura, they quickly vanish from his dream space. Suddenly, Natura's body stops twisting and jerking, and slowly relaxes. Natura returns to a sound sleep for the rest of the night.

At six o'clock sharp the next morning, the dark room suddenly lit up as if the sun itself had entered the room! Of course, the brilliant light could only be seen by Raziel and Natura. No human beings either inside or outside the house could see it. Only God and his angels had the ability to see such heavenly light.

"Rise and shine, Natura!" Raziel announced in his booming voice.

Suspended in front of a large blackboard on a wall, Raziel held a book in one hand and a piece of chalk in another. He certainly looked ready to begin the class. Natura gathered his textbook, notebook, and essay paper, and quietly floated to position himself near Raziel.

"Good morning Natura! I hope you slept well."

"Good morning, Archangel Raziel! No, I didn't sleep well. But thank you for asking."

Raziel knew, of course, that Natura hadn't slept well and the reason why. "Do you want to talk about it?"

"No thanks. I think I'm okay now. I just seemed to have some doubts in my dreams."

"I understand. It's nothing to worry about. It's only natural that you have some doubts, but as we complete your training, most doubts will disappear. Let's start with today's training. This morning I'll teach you about the character of Satan. It's extremely important that you understand the enemy you'll be fighting. Every guardian angel must know as much about Satan as he can if he's to win the many battles he'll have with him. Satan and his evil spirits are very cunning and tricky. They'll try everything in their evil textbooks to turn you against God and to get you to believe that evil is better than good. That's their job, their only job. Let's begin to learn a few things about Satan, which I'll call our 'Rules for Successful Battle'".

Raziel quickly turned around and wrote on the blackboard. "Rule Number 1: God's angels are always smarter than Satan because God created them to be smarter."

Turning to face Natura, Raziel boldly said with a very broad smile, "Now, Natura, let's talk about Rule Number 1. It's really the foundation of our ability to be exceptional angels. We'll always be smarter than Satan because God created us to be smarter. It's that simple. God is an all-powerful God and no spirit in this great Universe is more powerful. Remember that, Natura, and you'll always be a very smart and strong guardian angel!"

"Yes, sir! That's easy enough to remember."

"Very good." Raziel then turned to face the blackboard to write the next rule. "Rule Number 2: God is truly with you and for you always. No evil spirit can prevail against you if you believe this and call on God to help you."

Each time Raziel wrote a new rule on the board, he'd turn to Natura to read it, and then comment on it. As he did, he looked deep within Natura's spiritual body to be sure Natura understood the rule. He had an extraordinary ability to actually see the words as they vibrationally connected themselves to Natura's angelic brain.

Feeling assured that Natura understood Rule Number 2, Raziel turned to the blackboard and wrote the next rule, "Rule Number 3: God is more powerful than Satan."

"Now, this rule seems rather obvious, Natura," Raziel turned around to face Natura. "Very simply, if God wasn't more powerful than Satan, then God wouldn't be God, would He? Satan and his hosts of evil spirits attempted to overthrow God's kingdom at one time, and one time only. When they did, God and his army of angels defeated them. God then cast them out of heaven, down to the kingdom of this earthly world. Satan still has powers to do evil things in this world but can be overcome by God's power if we choose to use it. So, when Satan promises us we'll have powers if we worship him, it means we'll have powers to do evil rather than to do good. Do you understand this, Natura?"

Raziel looked intently at Natura as he spoke. Without even looking directly at Raziel, Natura could feel the look's laser-like sharpness pressing on his whole mind, body, and spirit.

"Yes, sir, I understand!"

"Rule Number 4 is this," Raziel began writing on the board. "Satan promises us knowledge of everything if we worship him."

"Now Natura, we have to consider that only God knows everything. He created the world, the heavens, and the entire universe, including all creatures. He even created Satan. Therefore, the creatures that God made can never know more than God, their Creator. It's just common sense. Satan promises us all-knowing knowledge but his promises are lies. When we believe Satan, we deceive ourselves by believing that we'll know as much as God knows. In a sense, Satan tells us that we can be our own 'God' and therefore we don't need the real God anymore. We remember the story of Adam and Eve when they disobeyed God by eating fruit from the tree of knowledge, or as some call it, 'the tree of good and evil'. Of course, God punished them by removing them from the Garden of Eden where they had everything, including a relationship with Him, and placing them in a world of hard work, suffering, pain, isolation, and even death."

Natura rubbed his forehead as if he was trying to rub-in the meaning of this rule which seemed to be at the heart of the battle between good and evil, darkness and light, harmony and disease, happiness and distress, and eternal life and death.

Observing Natura very closely as he always did, Raziel said, "Natura, I can tell that you're trying very hard to understand this very important rule. Don't worry so much about it now, it usually takes some time for it to sink-in. When it does, you'll then understand how important your job as a guardian angel will to help your humankind, John Muir, understand it as he grows up."

"Yes, sir! I can understand that it'll be important for John Muir to have great knowledge about all the natural things, but that it'll be equally as important for him to understand that God made them for our enjoyment and that we have a responsibility to take good care of them. He'll also learn that some evil people will oppose him because they want to use God's natural things for their own greedy and selfish benefit."

"How right you are, Natura!"

On and on, throughout the morning, Raziel followed this same pattern as he taught a total of seven rules to Natura, including Satan's promises of pleasure, peace, and possessions, such as wealth, property, and material things.

As the large clock in the tall tower at the end of High Street struck twelve noon, the huge bell in it rang loudly, twelve times in all, so everyone in the small town could hear it. Along the cobblestone street outside the house could be heard the sounds of horses pulling wagons, people pushing carts, merchants calling out attention to their wares, buyers haggling over prices, and people chatting and laughing. In the distance could be heard bagpipes as Scottish soldiers marched to their cadence as they practiced their drills on the parade grounds. These were the sounds Natura would become used to as he spent his first full day in Dunbar.

"Natura, let's take a long break. I want you to get outside and walk around the streets to learn your way around Dunbar. Be sure to take your Dunbar street map with you. Come back to this room in a few hours. And oh, one last thing. Keep yourself invisible so that no one can see you. I don't want you to scare people or get them all excited."

"Yes, sir!" Natura floated in a flash out the door, down the stairs, and out onto High Street to join the crowd of townspeople as they busily attended their daily affairs.

With his Dunbar street map in hand, he looked to his left and right, then at his map, to get his bearings. *"Which way should I go?"* He thought. It didn't seem to matter much, as long as he learned his way around Dunbar and found his way back. Still invisible to the townspeople, he slowly floated in the direction of the old Dunbar Castle and the town's two harbors. He was most familiar with this area since he and Raziel had flown over it as they landed in the little town. Taking a right turn onto Victoria Street, which leads down to the Cromwell Harbor, Natura weaved in and out among a steady stream of people coming from the fishing boats. Everyone had baskets filled with fresh fish they'd purchased from the fishermen. Seagulls fluttered overhead hoping to find any fish on the dock to which they could easily fly down and take for their own.

Moving slowly along the seawall, Natura now approached the outer, protective walls of old Dunbar Castle. He tried to imagine the fierce battles that took place around these walls over the centuries as the Scottish and English armies fought to include Dunbar in their kingdoms. Looking out across the vast North Sea, he could imagine that many ships bombarded the castle walls with their cannon balls while launching small boats filled with soldiers hoping to climb the castle's steep walls. He thought how futile their attempts were as they tried to enter such a secure fortress.

Trying to stay invisible, he hiked along the high cliffs overlooking the North Sea. He enjoyed the beautiful views and smelled the refreshing sea breezes, but soon had to return to the town's streets so he could learn them well. He looked up to see a street sign with the name Belhaven Road on it. Looking at his street map, he saw that this road would take him back to High Street from where he'd started his walk. Walking past a grammar school, and then a primary school, he thought for sure he'd see more of these buildings in the future as his humankind, John Muir, attended these schools. As he neared High Street, the streets became more crowded with horses pulling wagons and carriages as people went about their shopping or were just traveling from one place to another. He looked up and down the street for the Muir house. He was eager to return to the training being taught by Archangel Raziel.

*"That's the house."* Natura thought to himself. He quietly entered the front door so as not to disturb anyone in the house. Quickly, he floated up the stairs to the second floor and entered the darkened room where he knew Raziel was present.

"Good afternoon, Natura," Raziel's voice came from somewhere in the dark room.

Now seeing Raziel's eyes, Natura answered, "Good afternoon, Archangel Raziel!"

The room brightened as Raziel seemed to flip a light switch to light up the dark, dusty old room. Suspended in front of the black board once again, Raziel was prepared to resume the training.

"How was your first venture into Dunbar? Looks like you found your way back alright."

"Quite wonderful! I had a good flight down to the harbor, around the castle, along the seashore high above on the cliffs, and along the street where the two school houses are located. As I passed the schools, I thought that in the near future, my humankind, John Muir, will attend both schools. I will be there beside him to protect and guide him."

"Yes, indeed you will. But first we must train you well in how to battle the evil spirits so you can protect John Muir when he encounters evil spirits. Look at your training schedule and you'll see that you will complete this training by the end of this week. On Saturday, I've scheduled your examination event at the primary school's soccer field. So, let's get on with your training. I'll tell you more about your examination event on Friday of this week."

# CHAPTER 3

## Encounter with Satan

*""All these I shall give you, if you will prostrate yourself and worship me." Satan said. At this, Jesus said to him, "Get away, Satan! It is written: 'The Lord, your God, shall you worship and him alone shall you serve.'" Then the devil left him and, behold, angels came and ministered to him." Matthew 4:9-11*

During the week, Raziel continued to train Natura in how to battle evil spirits. Natura was a very good student and learned his lessons very well. But he was still a little nervous about his examination event. He had many doubts and questions. *Would he do well enough to pass the examination? Would he be able to put his training into practice? Why did Archangel Raziel call it an event? Most teachers simply call it an examination or just a final test."*

Now it was Friday afternoon and this week's training was winding down. Raziel erased the blackboard and then wrote on it 'Evil Spirit Examination Event'.

Raziel turned to Natura. "I know you've been wondering what this examination event is about. Tomorrow at sunrise, this event will be held in the soccer field behind the primary school. All of God's angels and all of Satan's evil spirits have been invited to attend. The highlight of the event will be your face-to-face meeting with Satan himself. Satan will try his best to convince you to follow him instead of following God as you do now. It will be up to you to decide either 'yes' or 'no'. But do not be afraid, because God's Holy Spirit is in you, always guiding you. He will tell you what to say and do. In addition, you can ask any archangel or guardian angel in attendance for their help. Never forget that God and His angels are always with you to help you. Also, Natura, you are a very gifted guardian angel and you have learned your lessons this week extremely well. You are well prepared to face Satan and any of his evil spirits. Do you have any questions?"

"No, Archangel Raziel. I can't think of any."

Natura couldn't think of any because he was too nervous to think. He was sort of overwhelmed with the thought of facing Satan.

"Very well, then. You're dismissed for the day. I'll see you at the soccer field tomorrow morning at six o'clock sharp, a little before the sun rises."

Raziel suddenly left the room. Where he went, Natura didn't know. He just knew Raziel was no longer in the room. Natura decided to go outside and float along the Dunbar streets again. He still had to learn his way around town. He needed some time to think about the examination event tomorrow morning. He left the room, slowly floated down the stairs, and exited the house. He decided to head in a new direction to see something different. He floated down High Street to Queens Road which led to the town of Berwick-upon-Tweed located a short distance away in England, just south of Dunbar. Of course, he didn't want to travel that far, although it was only about 28 miles. If he truly wanted to travel there, he could do it very quickly by putting his forward wing motion in the highest gear. He just needed to float around, see some new sights, and think about how he'd face Satan tomorrow.

Soon he passed Dunbar's post office and spotted a large church located behind it. As Natura floated closer to the old church, he read its name on a large sign, 'Dunbar Parish Church'. Made of local red sandstone, the church was built in 1821, only 17 years ago. Natura gazed at the beautiful stained-glass windows as he approached the front of the church. The large double doors were open and seemed to be inviting him to come inside.

Kneeling down at the back of the church, he decided to pray for courage and strength for tomorrow's event. He prayed, "Dear Lord, I know you are with me as I pray now. Thank you. I also know that you have made me to be a special guardian angel, and have instructed Archangel Raziel to train me well. He certainly has done that. Nevertheless, I'm still lacking in courage to face Satan tomorrow in the examination event. Please give me faith. Help me to have the faith that Jesus did when He was tempted by the devil in the desert for forty days. During my test, help me to call upon Your Name and also seek the help of my fellow angels who will attend the event. Thank you again. Amen."

Natura left the church and continued to venture around Dunbar. He now felt better and believed he was ready to face Satan and his evil spirits. On his return to the Muir house on High Street, he went up Countess Road until he'd reached the back of the primary school. He saw the soccer field where the examination event would be held. Floating onto the field, he looked around at the bleachers on both sides and imagined himself as a spiritual warrior facing Satan. He could hear the cheers and encouragement from his angel friends as he battled wits with Satan. Natura just hoped he would win the battle and pass his examination. Returning to his room, he went to bed and tried to dream of winning the battle.

However, Satan had other ideas. He ordered seven of his best demons, one each to represent the seven battle rules Raziel had taught Natura, to enter his dream space. As the demons had done the previous time, they were to pretend that they were his own dreams and to tell himself that he will be a failure as a guardian angel. For each of the seven rules, a demon would twist and change the rule to mean the very opposite of what Raziel had taught. For example, for Rule Number 3, a demon said, "God is not more powerful than Satan because God gave Satan power to rule over the kingdom of the Earth. Therefore, Satan controls all earthly things and creatures." In Natura's dream-state, he became confused because his own self-consciousness, or sense of self, had become trapped by the invasion of the seven evil spirits. He had become separated from his own awareness of what was good and what was evil. The battle within Natura's dream-space became very fierce as his good conscious fought against the evil conscious of the invading demons. As each of the seven demons presented a rule in direct opposition to Raziel's rules, Natura became more restless as he tried to sleep. His body began to twist and turn as he literally wrestled with the seven demons.

This time, however, Natura's dream conscious realized what was going on. It realized that evil spirits had once again entered Natura's dream space, so it quickly shielded his spirit behind a *faith* barrier. This made it impossible for the spirits to penetrate. Realizing that they'd lost this battle, they vanished from Natura's mind which allowed him to sleep well for the remainder of the night.

The next morning, Natura awoke early, stretched his arms, legs, and wings, and began to focus on the great event. He realized he'd not slept well but also realized that for some reason he felt victorious and spiritually stronger. His confidence seemed to have been strengthened during the night. He now felt ready to have his encounter with Satan.

Floating down to the soccer field, he saw the bleachers filled on both sides with many spirits, both good and evil. He, of course, spotted his best friend, Guardian Angel Harry, along with an army of spiritual warriors. Each warrior was proudly wearing a protective armor of *faith* over their entire body.

And then, Archangel Raziel stood in the middle of the field and announced, "Satan and Guardian Angel Natura, please come stand in front of me so we can begin this examination event."

Natura floated toward Raziel and suspended himself in front of him. All the angels cheered loudly to encourage Natura. Lightning and thunder interrupted their cheering as a fiery image streaked across the sky and entered the stadium. Sulfur-smelling smoke filled the atmosphere as Satan emerged from the blazing-hot center of the image to reveal himself. Total silence quickly fell on the entire stadium atmosphere. Everyone, including the angels, gazed quietly as Satan's feet burned a path on the grass as he partly walked and partly floated toward Raziel and Natura.

Now standing face to face with Natura, Satan tried to look friendly and non-threatening. He said, "Hello, Natura, glad to finally meet you. I've heard a lot about you. I'm here to invite you to join my kingdom. I will give you everything in this world that you desire. Just ask for it."

Natura stood tall as he gave careful thought to Satan's offer.

"No, thank you, Satan. You have some power and control over this earthly world, but someday it will end. I desire the things of Heaven."

"Very well, Natura. But you've only been told about Heaven by God. You have not actually seen it as you've seen things in this world. Look around you; all that you see in this world is real. Everything can be yours now for you to enjoy!"

"You're wrong Satan! I have seen Heaven! Now I'm seeing this earthly world. As I've already said, someday this world will end. All that is real in this world will be destroyed and return to dust. What God offers me in Heaven is also real and will last forever. It'll never be destroyed, for God has made it for us enjoy forever if we believe in Him and have faith."

"Okay, Natura. Then I'll offer you great worldly power. You can be in charge of half of my evil spirits and have lots of fun doing everything your own way. You don't have to listen to anyone nor be responsible for anything you do in your life."

"No, thank you, Satan. You know yourself that God has commanded us to love only Him, and to do unto others as we would have them do unto us. When we get to Heaven, we'll each be accountable to God for how well we did this on earth."

"Okay, Natura." Satan rolled his eyes, trying hard to offer Natura something else that'd convince him to accept evil, and to deny God and His goodness. He couldn't think of anything else.

Satan's face began to heat up. His eyes became very fiery. He looked ever so angry and threatening as he brought his face closer to Natura's face. Looking Natura steadily in the eyes, he hoped to scare Natura into changing his mind. For the longest time, Satan and Natura stood and faced each other. Sweat collected on

Natura's forehead. His head became very warm as Satan's eyes blazed, almost touching him.

Natura shouted, "I reject you, Satan, and all of your evil spirits!"

Suddenly Satan was no longer in Natura's face! But he was not totally gone. Looking around the soccer stadium, Natura saw that Satan had stopped to talk with one of his evil spirits. With his extra strong sense of hearing, Natura heard the conversation.

"Serpenta, I'm choosing you, among all of my finest evil spirits, to stay close to John Muir and seek every opportunity to tempt him to serve me instead of God. The best time to do this is when his guardian angel, Natura, is resting or is too busy with other things to notice your presence. Remember, you've been trained very well to do my evil work. I'm counting on you to succeed!" Satan's fiery eyes blazed with a burst of red-hot 'glowingness' and his big, wide mouth wrinkled with quivering, pulsing motions as red saliva seemed to foam between his lips.

"Yes, sir! You can count on me!" With that said, both Satan and Serpenta disappeared.

All of a sudden, cheers from all of the angels erupted! "Hooray for Natura! Hooray for Natura! He has won the battle of will and wits with Satan! He's now officially a Guardian Angel!"

Natura was stunned, still a bit shaky from the encounter with Satan. He felt a friendly arm wrap around his shoulders. Then many angelic friends encircled him to congratulate him.

"Well done, Natura," Guardian Angel Harry said as he squeezed Natura's shoulder. "I couldn't have done it better. All of us angels were praying for you!"

"Thanks, Harry, I could sense that all of you were praying for me. That certainly gave me much courage. I could also feel, and hear, the Holy Spirit within me telling me what to say. I'm glad it's over, at least for now. I know I'll always be tempted by Satan at certain times in my life. But now I know I can resist him. Thanks be to God, and all of my angelic friends!"

"You're very welcome, Natura, but always be watchful for Satan's evil spirits. He'll be forever watching and waiting for an opportunity to tempt John Muir, and to also persuade you to join his army of evil spirits. Before Satan disappeared, I saw him talking to one of his evil spirits. I think his name is Serpenta but I don't know anything about him. So, always be aware of his threat to you or to little Johnny."

"Yes, I also saw Satan talking to one of his evil spirits. I overheard their conversation as well. Now that I've seen him, I'll be watchful for him."

Archangel Raziel broke through the crowd of angels to offer Natura his congratulations.

"Well done, my dear angel! I knew you could do it! You've studied hard and you were well prepared. Now it's time for us to return to your training so you can be fully prepared to welcome John Muir into the world. You'll soon be busy as his guardian angel."

Natura and Raziel returned to the unoccupied second floor room above the living quarters of Daniel and Anne Muir. Over the next three months, Raziel continued to train Natura in the Scottish history and language, as well as everything about the world of nature. Each day, Natura floated through the streets of Dunbar to learn his way around. By the time John Muir was born, Natura was fully trained in everything he needed to know in order to be an excellent guardian angel.

# CHAPTER 4

## The Birth of John Muir

*"Before I formed you in the womb I knew you, before you were born I dedicated you, a prophet to the nations I appointed you." Jeremiah 1:5*

*"So valuable to heaven is the dignity of the human soul that every member of the human race has a guardian angel from the moment the person begins to be." St. Jerome*

The night before John Muir was born, Raziel completed his training of Natura and began to erase the large blackboard upon which he'd written many notes. He turned toward Natura. "Natura, this completes your training. You're now ready to be a guardian angel. Tomorrow morning around sunrise, the baby John Muir will be born. Immediately after his birth, I will perform a brief blessing ceremony to unite your angelic spirit with his human spirit. Congratulations!"

"Thank you, Archangel Raziel! I also believe I'm ready to be a guardian angel, thanks to your excellent teaching. I'm very happy that God chose me to be John Muir's guardian angel. I will work very hard to protect and guide him throughout his earthly life. I'm so excited to begin my work!"

"I can see that you are!" Raziel had an unusual big smile on his large face. He was always so serious about his work and didn't allow himself to smile or laugh very much. At this moment, Raziel was very proud of Natura for being such a good student. He knew in his heart that Natura would do an excellent job as John Muir's guardian angel.

"Well, it's been a long day of teaching and learning. Let's call it a day and get a good night's sleep." Raziel stretched his giant wings, yawned, and disappeared into a corner of the room to levitate for the rest of the night.

"Good night, sir," Natura said as Raziel's image quickly disappeared.

Natura gathered his notebooks, papers, and textbooks and stored them away in his angel backpack. He began to relax and get ready for bed, but he was very excited about the big birth event early tomorrow morning. He knew it'd be hard for him to fall asleep so he decided to read for a while from one of his nature textbooks. As he did, he settled down and dozed off to sleep. During the night, when some sounds on High Street would awaken him, he'd read some more until he went to sleep again. This went on most of the night. By early morning, around 4:00 a.m., he was sound asleep.

However, he was soon awakened by people talking and walking around in the room just below him. He knew that it was the bedroom of Daniel and Anne Muir. Up until now, they were very quiet and he hardly heard a peep from them once they went to bed each night. This morning was different. He heard the front door open and close rather loudly. Looking out the window, down onto High Street, he saw Daniel Muir hurriedly walking to the house directly across the street. It was the house of Margaret and David Gilrye, the parents of Anne Muir. Shortly after Daniel knocked loudly on the door, Natura saw a person open the door and greet Daniel. They talked very briefly. Afterward, Daniel turned and walked briskly toward the center of town.

"*Where was he going at this hour?*" Natura thought. Raziel was sleeping soundly; Natura could hear his angelic snoring, so he didn't want to awaken him.

Then Natura heard the voices of Daniel and Anne's two little daughters, Margaret and Sarah, as they gleefully entered their mother's bedroom. Natura could also hear the voices of two servants as they conversed with Anne Muir. All of a sudden, Natura realized that Anne must be in labor and would soon give birth to her third child, John Muir.

"Archangel Raziel," Natura called quietly. "I think Anne Muir is going into labor and will soon have her baby."

"Yes, I know, Natura," Raziel replied, as if a bit annoyed by being awakened. "If you wish, you can go down stairs to her bedside to observe and await the birth. I'll come down around sunrise because I know exactly when the baby will be born."

Angels knew that kind of information because God had told them. Raziel knew every detail that would happen during the birth, but at this point, Natura did not. God would tell him more as he learned to be a good guardian angel. That's just the way God works.

Natura slowly floated down the stairs and entered the hallway leading to Anne's and Daniel's bedroom. He was totally invisible to human beings but he had to be careful to be sure his hands, feet, and wings didn't make noises when they touched the floor and walls. The vibrational energy forces surrounding his invisible body always created sounds when they encountered such hard material in the earthly world.

The bedroom door was partly open. He saw little Margaret and Sarah on their mother's bed. The two servants were bringing hot water from the kitchen and pouring it into large hand-washing bowls located on the bedside tables. Several clean hand towels were placed next to the bowls. Anne Muir was talking to Margaret and Sarah.

"Now girls, soon I will give birth to your brother or sister because I'm now in labor. Remember what I told you about labor. It's the time when a pregnant mother begins to give birth to her baby. It's called labor because it can be hard work for a mother as the baby leaves her womb and enters the real world. Someday as you get older, you'll understand what this means. Your father has gone to fetch our doctor so he can help me deliver my baby. When he and the doctor return, I want you girls to go to your room until the servants come get you. Okay girls?"

"Yes, Mama," Margaret and Sarah said, almost at the same time. They each gave their mother a quick kiss on her cheek as she hugged them tightly. They then jumped from the bed, ran out the door, and down the hall to their bedroom.

The front door slowly opened as Margaret and David Gilrye arrived from across the street. They proceeded down the hall to Anne's bedroom.

"Anne, are you alright?" Margaret, Anne's mother, asked as she entered the bedroom. David followed close behind her.

"Yes, Mom, I'm fine now, but I know it's time for this baby to be born. I can feel the contractions getting more frequent. Thank you and Dad for coming over."

Margaret and David hung up their overcoats. Margaret rolled up her dress sleeves and washed her hands in one of the hand-washing bowls. David greeted Anne, kissed her on both cheeks, excused himself, and went to the large parlor, just down the hallway.

Soon the front door quickly opened. "Anne, we're back! Dr. McGregor is with me!" Daniel said excitedly as he breathed very hard. He and Dr. McGregor had literally run from his home to the Muir's home. They both entered the bedroom where Anne, Margaret, and the two servants were waiting.

"A very good morning to you, Anne and Margaret!" Dr. McGregor greeted them, and nodded a hello to the two lady servants. He carefully looked around the bedroom and particularly at the towels and bowls of hot water sitting on the night stands. "I see that everything is ready for your baby's delivery. If this birth is anything like the births of Margaret and Sarah, you'll be just fine, as will the baby."

Dr. McGregor removed his coat, rolled up his shirt sleeves, and thoroughly washed his hands in one of the hand-washing bowls. He opened his large, black doctor's bag and removed a few instruments and some medication he'd need for the baby's delivery. He placed them on a clean towel on one of the bedside tables.

By this time, Daniel still had his overcoat on and paced impatiently around the bedroom, praying out loud to God for a healthy baby and wife. His praying and pacing made everyone else in the room very nervous. They could hardly concentrate on helping Anne.

Finally, Dr. McGregor grew impatient and said, "Daniel, you can help me and Anne the most by being quiet and still. If you must move to another room in your home to do this, then please do so."

A bit shaken, and of course, embarrassed, Daniel gave everyone a stunned look, bowed his head, and slowly excited the bedroom. He walked down the hallway and joined his father-in-law, David, in the large parlor.

The drama in Anne's and Daniel's bedroom was just beginning.

"Now, Anne, let's take a look at the progress of your birth." Dr. McGregor lifted the covers to examine Anne very closely. As he did, he shook his head slightly, frowned, replaced the covers over Anne, and gently held her hands in his.

"Anne, my dear, this is going to be a difficult delivery. Your baby wants to enter this world feet first instead of head first. But just be patient and everything should go very well. It'll just take more time and care. So, for now, I want you to stop trying so hard to deliver the baby, if you can."

Anne looked at Dr. McGregor and nodded. She tried to relax and not push the baby as hard. Dr. McGregor carefully placed his hands-on Anne's stomach area to place pressure on the baby's head and upper body. As he did, Natura stepped up next to him and placed his hands over the doctor's hands to assist. Natura looked inside Anne's body and saw the baby's body. Angels are given special senses for doing this. With that advantage, Nature was able to direct and guide the doctor's hands in the right way to help the baby be delivered more easily and safely. Dr. McGregor, of course, didn't realize he was being helped by Natura but he did think what a great job he was doing to position the baby's body for easier delivery. He was amazed at himself!

As the baby's body became better positioned for delivery, Dr. McGregor said, "Now Anne, you can begin pushing again, but not too hard. I'll hold onto the baby's feet and gently help you deliver it."

Working together, Anne pushing, Dr. McGregor carefully pulling, and Natura gently pressing on Anne's stomach walls, the baby slowly came into the world, feet first instead of head first.

"It's a boy!" Dr. McGregor announced. "Congratulations, Anne, you now have a healthy baby boy!"

He held the little baby up for Anne to see. She beamed with joy, and relief! Tears of joy ran down her cheeks! Dr. McGregor very carefully held the baby for a moment; then he gently spanked the baby's bottom to prompt him to take his first breath of air.

"Wahh! Wahh! Wahh!" the newborn baby cried. Dr. McGregor handed the baby to one of the servants for washing and wrapping.

Hearing the baby's cry, Daniel and David returned to the bedroom, saw the servants attending to the baby boy, and kissed Anne on the forehead. Daniel said, "Congratulations, my dear! You did it! Now we have a new son to go with our two little daughters. Oh, let us say a prayer to thank God for this wonderful gift!"

Daniel prayed out loud, looked up toward Heaven, and clasped his hands over his heart. "Thank you, Almighty God, for this gift of a baby boy whose name will be John Muir! We dedicate him to You and to Your service. Amen."

Archangel Raziel had entered the room just before the birth. Natura could see him but no humans could. Natura knew that Raziel was there to perform a brief blessing ceremony of binding John Muir's human spirit with his own angelic spirit so that Natura could spiritually become John's guardian angel.

"Natura," Raziel said, "please place your hands over John Muir's heart and repeat after me. "John Muir, I now bind your spirit with mine and promise to protect and guide you all the days of your life."

As Natura repeated those words, he felt an unusual spiritual energy flow between John's body and his body. Raziel spread his giant wings to surround both Natura and little John, and simply said, "So be it, according to God's good wishes. From this moment until the end of John Muir's earthly life, Natura is officially assigned to be his guardian angel. Congratulations, Natura!"

Now truly feeling like a new guardian angel, Natura rested in Raziel's warm and soft wings while John Muir rested in his mother's arms. Soon, Natura was alone with Daniel and Anne Muir, baby John, his grandparents, and the two servants. He knew that

Raziel had quietly and gracefully departed the earth's atmosphere and returned to Heaven to do his other archangel work.

"Go get Margaret and Sarah so they can see their new baby brother!" Daniel said to one of the servants. "And light the candles in the front windows to announce to all of Dunbar that we have a new baby. Invite the neighbors in for tea and cookies, and a prayer meeting to celebrate with us the birth of John Muir."

Margaret and Sarah quickly ran into the bedroom. Then they suddenly stopped. Slowly and quietly, they approached their mother as she held their baby brother. "See, your new baby brother, girls. You can give him a soft kiss on his forehead if you like." They did. What joy shown on their faces as they looked in disbelief at their new brother, John.

Knocks on the front door by visiting neighbors could be heard throughout the day. Neighbor after neighbor came to the house to congratulate Daniel and Anne on their son's birth. They also brought gifts of food to help feed the Muir's for a week or so. Some also brought gifts of clothing for the new baby boy. Daniel invited the neighbors into the large parlor where he continued his prayer meeting all day. Frequently, he'd stop preaching and lead everyone in hymn singing as he joyfully played his homemade fiddle.

As the afternoon became later, Margaret Gilrye gently reminded Daniel and the neighbors that Anne and baby John needed to rest, and urged them to end the celebrations and prayer meeting.

David Gilrye stood by the bedside of Anne and looked down at his handsome grandson sleeping in her arms. "Little Johnny, you and I have a lot of wandering to do. I have much I want to teach you about life and nature. Rest for now, but grow up quickly so we can begin our wanderings. I can't wait!"

And precisely at this time, the idea of wandering was first expressed by David Gilrye. Little did he know that little Johnny would one day become one of the world's greatest natural wanderers and make a remarkable impression on mankind the idea of conserving the Earth's natural wonders.

Natura proudly observed the activities and heard the conversations all day long. He had already begun his responsibilities as a guardian angel and carefully watched over little Johnny. Being a spiritual being, Natura especially watched for any signs of Satan and his evil spirits who might venture into the house to harm John. Natura also could see into the future of John Muir's life and knew the obstacles he would face. However, he was confident that, with God's help, he would help John realize his destiny.

"Don't be so sure of yourself, Natura!" A spirit voice came from somewhere nearby.

Looking around with his angelic spirit eyes, Natura saw an evil spirit hovering near him. He knew that it must be Serpenta who was assigned by Satan to scare him away from his guardian angel duties and also to prevent John Muir from becoming the great naturalist God wanted him to be.

"I am sure of myself, Serpenta! I believe that's your name although we haven't been formally introduced. I only know a little about you and your assignment from Satan to derail John Muir's purpose in life. I am very prepared to protect John and guide him toward his destiny. It will be my pleasure to battle you at any time and defeat you. If I need help in doing that, be assured, God's army of spiritual warriors stand ready to join with me."

"Just hold on a minute, Natura! You're getting all worked up when you don't have to. You can avoid any battles by joining forces with Satan. You'll have a blast! Besides what's one human soul like John Muir worth when you can have the whole world to enjoy?"

"Serpenta, one human soul is *everything* to God! All souls are special to Him. He'll do all that He can not to lose even one of them!

"I can see we're getting nowhere with this conversation, Natura. Let's agree to disagree. And let us both be prepared to meet again when you least expect it!" Serpenta's image vanished from Natura's view. He knew Serpenta had departed. Every evil spirit quickly departs when they know you can't be 'won over' with their words. Natura knew that the next time he encountered Serpenta, it would be a real battle, either of wits or by physical force.

# CHAPTER 5

## Early Learning Years

*"I loved to wander in the fields to hear the birds sing, and along the seashore to gaze and wonder at the shells and seaweeds, eels and crabs in the pools among the rocks when the tide was low; and best of all to watch the waves in awful storms thundering on the black headlands and craggy ruins of the old Dunbar Castle when the sea and the sky, the waves and the clouds, were mingled together as one....My earliest recollections of the country were gained on short walks with my grandfather when I was perhaps not over three years old." John Muir (3)*

Little John Muir steadily grew up with the help of his parents, grandparents, sisters, and servants. And yes, Natura was always at John's side to protect and guide him. He carefully watched over him day and night, as John's family cared for him as a baby, taught him to walk and talk, and prepared him to start school once he was old enough. Each family member, as well as the servants, taught John different things and influenced his personality development in special ways.

John's mother, Anne, was naturally his primary teacher, as she spent much of her time caring for him in every way. Nursing, bathing, dressing, cuddling baby John several times a day made Anne very happy. She delighted in tenderly caring for her first-born son. Her two little daughters, Margaret and Sarah, ages four and two, still required much care and frequent attention, so she had her hands full. However, as they grew older, they were always eager and able to help care for their baby brother, John.

As Anne nursed baby John, she talked to him as only a mother can. "Little John, you're the handsomest boy in all of Scotland! I'm so blessed to have you, as well as your two sisters, and of course, your father," she would frequently say. And like all mothers, she'd sing lullabies and hymns as she rocked him to sleep. Quite often, she'd sing some old Scottish ballads she'd learned as she grew up.

Anne had a wonderful sense of humor and would often laugh out loud when John made funny faces, as he sometimes did to avoid eating his mashed green peas. "Now, John," she'd say while laughing, "you have to eat some vegetables. I declare, there are enough peas on your face to feed our whole family!"

Daniel, John's father, also had a gift for music. He had a fine tenor voice and sang while he worked. He'd often join in the singing of Scottish ballads at neighborhood gatherings. But most of all, Daniel had a special talent and love for playing a fiddle. Early in his life, he was so eager to play a fiddle that he made one of his own. The night he finished it he was so excited to play it that he ran ten miles through wind, rain, and mud to the nearest village store to buy fiddle strings. (4) However, Daniel's love of religion far exceeded his love of music. Eventually, he became so devoted to his fundamentalist Christian faith that it became the most important thing in his life. And he expected it to be the most important thing in his family's life too!

As Anne finished bathing baby John one day, Daniel came into the house to get a fresh bucket of drinking water for his store's customers. He said, "Anne, don't forget we have our family prayer meeting promptly at six o'clock this evening in the parlor room. Remind Margaret and Sarah to learn their Bible verse and be ready to recite it at the meeting. And be sure to bring baby John to the meeting; it's not too soon for him to start hearing the word of God!"

"Yes, dear!" She knew how important these prayer meetings were to Daniel and how much he insisted that the children learn the Bible. Daniel thought the Bible was the only book a person needed from birth to the grave. Like every good Scottish wife, Anne wanted to please her husband in all things, even when Daniel's religious expectations seemed somewhat extreme. (5)

Anne and Daniel had one joy in common besides their children. (6) Behind their house was a large garden, surrounded by a high stone wall. Pear and apple trees clung to the stone walls while spreading elm trees and boxwood hedges lined the pathways. Daniel delighted in gathering and planting choice plants and flowers in the garden. Anne and the children also delighted in them. Every day, Anne would take the children on a walk through the beautiful garden and call out the names of plants and flowers so the children could begin learning about them.

"Children, look at the wonderful plot of lilies your father helped your Aunt Margaret Rae plant," she said one day as she walked in the garden. "Aren't their trumpet-shaped white flowers the prettiest of all the flowers in the garden!"

Natura, of course, was also delighted with the garden's many trees, plants, and flowers. As he walked beside Anne and the children, he would sometimes blow on certain plants and flowers to cause them to move. When they did, they would catch the eye of Anne who'd then point them out to the children. Natura knew how important it was to begin teaching John about nature's trees, plants, and flowers. He wanted to help guide John however he could; he thought the walled garden was a good place to start.

Perhaps John's Grandfather Gilrye influenced him the most toward learning about nature. John's earliest memories of nature was when his grandfather took him on walks around Dunbar. One of his first outings was to Lauderdale Park located only a short walk from their homes on High Street. (6)

"Okay John, let's put on your coat, hat, and gloves for our walk. It's a little nippy outside and the winds from the North Sea are blowing hard against the seawalls," his grandfather said.

With a little help from his mom, John put on his coat, hat, and gloves. He went to the front door to wait on his grandfather to open it.

"John, hold tightly to your grandfather's hand when you cross any streets," his mother said. "And do be careful playing in the park lest you fall and hurt yourself."

"Yes, Mama, I will."

"Don't worry Anne, I'll take very good care of my only grandson. And I'm sure little John will take good care of me. Won't you John?" He now stood next to John and looked down at him. John looked up at him and thought his grandfather was the tallest person in the world!

Grandfather opened the front door; he and John walked out onto High Street. Many townspeople were busy going and coming from the market place. Those who knew Grandfather Gilrye greeted him and looked smilingly at his grandson. The weather was 'a little nippy' as Grandfather had said, but the sun was shining brightly. They proceeded to walk north on High Street. Natura, of course, also went along. Still invisible to people, he was always nearby John at all times to protect and guide him. In the distance could be seen old Dunbar Castle as its crumbling walls looked out at the North Sea. Soon they were at the corner of High Street and Bayswell Road where Lauderdale Park was located.

As they entered the park, Grandfather Gilrye said, "Now John, let's go over to that fig tree growing against that sunny wall and get a few figs to taste."

When they got to the tree, John's grandfather lifted him onto his shoulders. John's little legs straddled his grandfather's neck. "Reach up and get you one of the biggest figs."

As he tried to lift John higher, his right leg weakened and he began to fall. Serpenta quietly hovered nearby looking for any opportunity to disrupt or interfere with John's learning about nature. With a flash, he flew next to Grandfather to place pressure on him to cause him to fall. In doing so, he knew that John would also fall. He hoped that both he and his Grandfather would be hurt and have to return home.

Natura instantly saw Serpenta's negative energy field next to Grandfather Gilrye and said in his angelic voice, "Serpenta, stop in the name of God! Or I'll propel my sharp energy through you until you dissolve into nothing!"

"As you request, Natura. You've won this battle but rest assured there'll be more to follow." Serpenta knew he was in danger of being killed by Natura's superior strength and weaponry. He quickly vanished into nowhere, far out of reach of Natura's energy field, he hoped. Seeing Serpenta's departure, Natura quickly braced his angelic body against Grandfather Gilrye and covered John with his large wings to hold him steady. Grandfather Gilrye was able to grab a limb on the large fig tree to steady himself.

"Whew, good grab, huh John!" Grandfather managed not to fall. He, of course, thought his grabbing the tree limb saved him from falling; he was unaware of Natura's help and the presence of the demon Serpenta. Natura was happy to help because that was part of his responsibility as John's guardian angel.

"How'd that fig taste, John?"

"Yummy!" John had lots of fig juice dripping from his little chin.

"Look at those apples!" Grandfather pointed toward the small apple orchard at the far end of the park. "Let's go pick a few, taste them, and take some home to your mother and sisters."

As grandfather and John strolled through the park, grandfather pointed out different flowers and plants to John to help him learn their names. Natura was also helpful as he blew aside a few of the thicker bushes to reveal other plants growing behind them. Grandfather Gilrye also pointed to and called the names of different birds resting in the trees and bushes.

After an hour or so in the park, John and his grandfather started toward home. On their way, Grandfather Gilrye pointed with his cane to shop signs to call out different letters for John to learn. He also pointed out the numerals on the large clock dial, high on the Town Hall tower, and taught John how to tell time. (8) John was a very quick learner and remembered most everything his grandfather taught him.

On another walk one day, Grandfather Gilrye took John to a hayfield to explain how hay was grown, harvested, and bailed. When they stopped to rest on one of the haycocks, John heard a sharp cry from somewhere inside the haycock. Eagerly jumping up, John said, "Grandpa, I hear a wee crying sound in the haycock!" (9)

"You hear only the wind, my boy." Grandfather's hearing was not that good because of his old age. But John insisted and began to dig into the hay with his little hands, turning the hay over until he discovered the source of the sound. There in the middle of the haycock was a mother field mouse with half a dozen of her young babies hanging onto her teats.

"Look grandfather! I told you I heard something!" John removed more hay to totally uncover the mother and her babies.

It truly was an exciting nature discovery for John! Although the mother and babies were startled, they hardly moved before John placed some hay over them.

"There, now you can enjoy your mother's milk without being disturbed," he said looking at the little babies as they hungrily sucked on their mother's teats.

As John grew older, his grandfather took him on longer walks. He often took him to the harbor to see the fishing boats as they came into the harbors with their loads of fish from the North Sea. (9) From the waterfront, John looked out at the North Sea as it met the Firth of Forth to see large sailing ships waiting for the wind to carry them up the huge inlet to Edinburgh to unload their cargo. From there, they'd load other outgoing cargo and sail away to other cities in Europe and around the world.

Although time seemed to pass slowly, John quickly grew in size and abilities. His family and Natura taught him very well, but like all children, he needed to attend school to get the best education. When he reached the age of three, he was ready to start school.

# CHAPTER 6

## Early Schooling Years

*"Old-fashioned Scotch teachers spent no time in seeking short roads to knowledge, or in trying any of the new-fangled psychological methods so much in vogue nowadays... We were simply driven pointblank against our books like soldiers against the enemy, and sternly ordered, 'Up and at 'em. Commit your lessons to memory!' If we failed in any part, however slight, we were whipped; for the grand, simple, all-sufficing Scotch discovery had been made that there was a close connection between the skin and the memory, and that irritating the skin excited the memory to any required degree." John Muir. (11)*

When John was around three years old, his sisters Margaret and Sarah walked with him to the Davel Brae primary school. With a little green bag containing his first book hanging around his neck, so he would not lose it, John gazed at the high walls around the schoolyard as they approached the school. Natura, of course, followed close behind, ever vigilant, watching every step John made and scanning the immediate surroundings for any dangers that might harm John.

Stopping at the large main entrance doors, Margaret and Sarah released John's hands. "Now John," Margaret said, "Sarah and I will return to pick you up this afternoon around 3:10 p.m. Please wait for us. Don't try to walk home by yourself. Mother wants the three of us to stay together going and coming from school."

"Okay, Margaret." HIs eyes were intently focused on the many children running and playing, obviously having a great time inside the large schoolyard. He couldn't wait to join them in the fun!

"And remember, John," Sarah, his younger sister, said, thinking she needed to instruct him, perhaps as a 'little mother', "don't be afraid. Be brave, stand your ground, and work hard to learn your first book well. Margaret and I will be just a short block down the road at the grammar school if you should need us."

"Sounds good, Sarah." John hurriedly turned and raced through the double-wide, opened doors toward the middle of the playground.

John quickly joined several boys playing kickball. Waiting for a turn to kick the ball, he recognized a few boys who lived near his house on High Street. They sometimes played kickball together in a narrow alleyway next to John's house.

"Okay, Johnny Muir, try your foot in kicking the ball," a neighbor boy, named Robert, said as he passed the soccer ball to John.

Although John was only three years old, he was taller than most boys his age. Looking around at the other boys, John squared his shoulders, put a very serious look on his face, and positioned himself to kick the ball. Already aware that other boys would naturally judge him on how well he did, John came at the ball with his right leg stretched well behind him, brought it forward to meet the ball in its center, and followed through with a reasonably good kick for a three-year-old. The ball soared over the heads of the boys waiting downfield, thanks in part to Natura who intervened a little by blowing the ball upward.

"Wow, Johnny Muir, what a kick!" Robert shouted. Most of the boys standing around seemed to agree. There was one exception. Michael, a four-year-old, was already a good soccer player; he observed John's kick with a frown on his face. He was the self-proclaimed best soccer ball kicker in primary school. A few of his friends agreed with him. So, the rest of the boys thought it must be true.

Feeling somewhat victorious after his fine kick, John stepped back to retrieve his little green bag which he'd laid on the ground so he could freely kick the ball. As John raised up and placed the bag cords around his neck, Michael walked up to him, placing his face very close to John's face. Michael's self-opinioned position among the boys had been threatened by John's extra good kick.

"Well, so you're John Muir!" Michael glared at John. "And you think you're such a good kicker, do you?"

As Michael spoke, Mungo Siddons, the schoolmaster, rang the school bell, signaling that classes would soon begin.

John turned his face from Michael and began to walk toward the school house. Michael shouted to John so every boy around could hear him, "If you think you're so good, meet me after school at the top of Davel Brae hill! I'll show you which of us is the toughest!"

John only partly listened because his thoughts were now focused on finding his classroom. He also knew Scottish boys were naturally very competitive and quickly settled any ranking disputes with a fist fight or a good wrestling match after school. He wasn't worried. He knew he could take care of himself. Natura watched very closely, and of course, heard Michael's threats, or maybe they were just boyish challenges. Whatever, he'd be right beside John to protect him, and also help him, however he could.

John was assigned a seat near thc middle of the classroom. Students were busy finding their assigned seats. They were also busy talking, and continued their excited chatter as they'd done on the playground. Mungo Siddons observed for only a moment, then raised his traditional schoolmaster stick, struck his desk with a powerful force as he calmly roared, "Silence!"

Amazingly, an eerie silence settled over the room. "Welcome, students, to our first day of school. And listen to me very carefully; I will use this stick on your bottoms rather frequently if you fail to listen and follow my instructions! You will not hear another warning from me. You'll only feel this stick. Understood?"

Almost in unison, every student replied with a resounding, "Yes sir, Mungo Siddons!"

John had no trouble at all reading and spelling his way through the first little book. He knew his letters very well because his grandfather had taught them to him by pointing them out on shops signs as they walked around town. And, of course, John had an excellent memory!

All very quickly it seemed, John's first day of primary school came to a close. He gathered his first primary book along with his homework instructions and placed them in his little green bag. Upon dismissal from school, he slowly walked to the schoolyard entrance doors to wait for Margaret and Sarah. He'd already forgotten about Michael's challenge to him to meet at Davel Brae hill after school to settle their differences. Oftentimes, that was the case with boyish threats made on the school grounds.

As John waited for Margaret and Sarah, he looked across Belhaven Road toward the sea wall. He saw the waves as they changed into large white swells attempting to climb over the high, rocky walls. Their rushing, pounding sounds were like beautiful music to John's ears. He never tired of hearing them. They reminded him of life itself, always active, always moving, always alive with endless energy.

"And how was your first day at school, John?" Margaret asked as she and Sarah walked up to him. "Yes, John, how was it?" Sarah also asked.

"Well, it was very good! I kicked some good soccer balls on the playground, and in class, I spelled every word in today's lessons."

"Good job, John!" Margaret said. "Let's hurry home so we'll have a longer time to play!"

Margaret and Sarah grabbed John's hands as they walked down the road toward High Street. Soon the three of them began to skip. The girls laughed as they occasionally lifted John by his arms and swung his feet high into the air.

Natura followed closely behind them. He thought, *"Well, I also had a good day at school, watched my little John very closely, and helped him a bit when he made that great kick. I even learned how to spell a few new words."*

As John, Margaret, and Sarah walked up Davel Brae hill, they'd planned to race down the other side to see who'd be first to reach their home. Near the top of the hill, they saw five little boys huddled together as if waiting for them to arrive.

"Hey, look Margaret and Sarah," John said, "there's my friend Michael and four other friends."

"Hello, Michael," John said, waving his hands over his head. "What are you guys doing up here?"

"Well, well," Michael sort of stammered a bit, seeing that John was accompanied by Margaret and Sarah. "I was just thinking that you and me could have a wrestling match to see who's the strongest boy in our classroom."

Not intimidated nor afraid at all, John quickly placed his book bag on the ground and said, "Okay with me, Michael. I'm always ready for a good wrestling match!"

Margaret stepped between them. Then Sarah did the same. Margaret said, "Now boys, wrestling is no way to solve any problems. Instead, you should play a game to see who's the smartest. Why don't you agree to have a spelling bee or a math problem-solving contest?"

As John and Michael stood ready to wrestle, Natura moved into position between them to ensure that the match was a fair one, and also ensure that neither boy got injured. However, as the boys stood face to face, they sort of lost their interest in wrestling. It just didn't seem the right place and time to do it. Besides the boys were very eager to get home to eat some treats and have fun playing. The idea of wrestling passed from their minds as do many great ideas that three and four years have at this time in their lives. Michael and his friends soon turned around and headed for their homes.

Michael, however, had to say some parting words. "Hey, Johnny Muir, we'll see you tomorrow at school!"

"Okay, Michael." It's as if the two boys had simply forgotten why they were going to have a wrestling match.

Natura gave a sigh of relief. However, he was ready to help if he was needed, especially if his arch-enemy, Serpenta, showed to up to give Michael any advantage in the wrestling match.

Reaching their home, they flung open the door of their house, greeted their father who was busy waiting on his customers in his grain and food store, and ran upstairs to tell their mother all about their school day.

"John, how was your first day at school?" She asked.

"I had a wonderful day, Mama! I played kickball with my friends, swung on the playground swings, and won five marbles playing marbles. I must say I'm a pretty good marble player!"

"Yes, I'm sure you are, John. And how well did you do in your classroom?"

"Very well, I think. I could spell all of the words correctly in our first book. Grandfather had already taught me all of my letters so I could read every sign on High Street. It was very easy for me to spell today."

Likewise, his mother asked Margaret and Sarah how their school day went. John excused himself. "Mama, I'm going over to Grammy's and Grandpa's house to study my lessons, okay?"

"Yes, John. But mind that you don't eat too much of your grandmother's caraway-seed cakes and ruin your supper."

"Yes, mam!" John ran toward the stairs. He knew that Grandmother Gilrye always had lots of homemade cakes and other treats for Margaret, Sarah, and him to eat after school.

Natura floated over John as he ran down the stairs, through his father's store, out the front door, and across the street to Grandfather and Grandmother Gilrye's house. Hastily knocking on their front door, John quickly opened it, rushed into the kitchen where he knew his grandmother would be, and without a word, embraced her from behind before she had time to turn around.

"My little Johnny Muir! Why, I just knew it was you! Who else would give me such a greeting at this hour?"

"Are you hungry, my boy? I've got lots of cakes, scones, and fresh blackberry jam!" She turned to give John a big hug. She then quickly placed several plates filled with fresh homemade treats on the kitchen table.

"Thanks Grammy!" John quickly but politely filled a plate with delicious treats.

"You're so very welcome, Johnny! I'll get you a big glass of milk to wash it down."

Soon, John had filled his stomach with his grandmother's treats. "Thanks, Grammy, everything was just yummy! Where's Grandpa?"

John carried his empty plate and glass to the sink for his grandmother to clean.

"He's outback in the garden tending to his plants and flowers." She took his dishes and placed them in the sink. "I think he's also feeding the birds."

"What fun! I'll go help him." He ran toward the back door that opens to a large garden. His grandfather was busy near the middle of the garden filling the bird feeders with seeds.

"Can I help? Can I help, Grandpa?" John ran to where he was standing.

"You certainly can, Johnny!" He handed John a scoop of seeds for him to pour into a bird feeder. "After we fill the feeders, let's sit on this bench and watch the birds eat. We'll play our bird-naming game to see who can name the most birds!"

John's grandfather had already taught him the names of many birds and how to identify them with their feather markings, their wings and tail shapes, and of course, their unique vocal sounds. When he and his grandfather played their bird-naming game, he proudly called out their correct names.

Pointing his finger, John said, "There's a brown-thrasher! And there's a blue-jay! Over in the tree in the far corner is a wren!"

"What kind of wren, Johnny?"

"It's a Bewick's Wren, because it has a white edge around its tail feathers."

"Right you are, Johnny! Good job!"

John's grandfather knew his grandson had a very special gift for naming birds. Each time John visited his grandfather's house, and when the two of them went for long walks, his grandfather would teach him the names of additional birds.

"Come on, Johnny, let's take a stroll through the garden. I want to show you my newest plants and flowers."

The two of them slowly walked through the large garden, stopping now and then for grandfather to show and teach John the names of different plants, flowers, and trees, even a few insects. And like his talent for naming different birds, John had a special ability to remember the names of different 'all things natural', as his grandfather called them. During their long nature walks, the two of them spent much time naming them. This was the beginning of John's interest in nature. He dearly loved learning about nature from his grandfather and knew in his heart that he'd always have a special relationship with nature.

Natura floated just above the heads of John and his grandfather. Knowing everything in the natural world as he did, he was so proud of John.

Stopping at a newly planted tree in a corner of the garden, John's grandfather asked him the name of the tree. During a recent walk in Lauderdale Park, grandfather had shown him the same type tree, explained its tree form and leaf shape, and cone-like fruit.

"Johnny, do you remember the name of this tree?" His grandfather gently held one of its branches with leaves in his large hands.

John touched one of the egg-shaped leaves, turned it over to study it very closely, and looked at the dark gray bark of the tree trunk. Natura wanted to help, but he was careful not to make his help too obvious. Natura saw the little cone-like fruit next to the leaf John was holding. He gently blew across John's hand, which caused a slight tickling on his hand. This brought John's attention to it. John smiled brightly as the fruit helped him remember the name of the tree.

He looked up at his grandfather. "Why, it's a gray alder, Grandpa! Don't you remember?"

"Right you are, Johnny! Yes, I remember. I'm so happy that you remembered! You're learning that every plant, flower, and tree, all-natural things, have many parts that help identify their names."

They continued their stroll through the garden. Besides the beautiful garden behind John's own house, grandfather's garden was one of prettiest gardens in all of Dunbar. Soon they approached the house's back door that led directly into the kitchen. They could hear John's grandmother and his two sisters, Margaret and Sarah, happily talking in the kitchen. The girls were enjoying some of grandmother's cakes and scones just as John had done earlier.

Opening the door and entering, grandfather greeted Margaret and Sarah. "Welcome, my two prettiest granddaughters! I see you're enjoying your grandmother's delicious cakes and scones! Eat all you want so I don't have to eat them all later."

About 5:00 p.m., the children's mother entered the house, greeted her parents, and reminded the children to study their school lessons before returning home for supper.

"After supper, your father will have our nightly worship service in the parlor."

Their father, Daniel, was very strict on the children in every way. In particular, he was a very stern religious man. When the family gathered for a meal around the table, Daniel expected everyone to talk only when necessary, because to him, the meal was a sacred time for worship and thanksgiving to God in itself.

After supper, the Muir family gathered in the large parlor for worship, including Bible study, prayer, and hymn singing. The children had daily worship assignments. Each child had to memorize a few Bible verses and a few lines of a hymn every day. During their evening worship time, they had to stand up and recite them. By the time John was eleven years old, he could recite the New Testament and three-fourths of the Old Testament.

# CHAPTER 7

## Fighting and Thrashings

*"An exciting time came when at the age of seven or eight I left the auld Davel Brae school for grammar school. Of course, I had a terrible lot of fighting to do, because a new scholar had to meet every one of his age who dared to challenge him, this being the common introduction to a new school. It was very strenuous for the first month or so, establishing my fighting rank, taking up new studies, especially Latin and French, getting acquainted with new classmates and the master and his rules... When we were fortunate as to finish a fight without a black eye, we usually escaped a thrashing at home and another next morning at school...A good double thrashing was the inevitable penalty, but all without avail; fighting went on without the slightest abatement, like natural storms; for no punishment less than death could quench the ancient inherited belligerence burning in our pagan blood." John Muir. (12)*

Quite often, during school recess or after school each day, the boys would choose opposing teams, or 'armies' as they sometimes called themselves, to decide who were the toughest boys in school. It took only a stare or a challenging word from either team to start the battle. Fist fighting, kicking, wrestling, gouging, and any other bruising, bodily encounters were considered acceptable. When both sides were thoroughly exhausted, sweating, and sorely bruised, someone who was getting the worst of the battle would yell, "If you've had enough, then we've had enough. We'd better get home before we all get into trouble!" And the hard-fought battle was ended on somewhat of a peaceful note until the two armies met again, perhaps the very next day. (13)

When John was seven or eight, he entered grammar school. On the second day of school, John was faced with a challenge from a tough boy named Wallace, who made fun of John's last name, Muir.

"Well, I tell you what, John," Wallace said, standing in front of his 'little gang of friends', your last name is not true Scottish! Not one of us has ever heard the name 'Muir' ever before in our grand Scottish history books. You must be from merry-old England, that backward nation to our south! If you're true Scottish, then you'll have to prove it to us!"

John's grandparents and parents had taught him that the Muir family belonged to the Scottish Gordon clan who had their original home in northeastern Scotland near Inverness. John was told that his great-grandfather, John Muir I, had married an English woman. (14) Although this made him part English in heritage, he still considered himself to be Scottish. As the many wars between Scotland and England resulted in fairly frequent boundary changes, the intermarriages between the Scots and English were very common.

His grandparents and parents had also taught him that bullying can sometimes be a problem in school. Bullying happens when someone stronger than you calls you names or threatens to harm you unless you do what they want you to do. John was told that when you ignore such people, they'll usually stop bullying you. However, if someone persists in a bullying behavior, then be brave and stand up to the bullying person as best as you can. If that doesn't work, ask for help from an adult.

John was tall for his age and was not easily intimidated. He'd already had his share of fights and thrashings in his short life. These fighting experiences had already made him into a very tough boy. He didn't blink or flinch when Wallace issued his challenge. He simply decided to stand up to Wallace and stepped forward. Now face to face with Wallace, John positioned his arms and legs for a fight, and waited for Wallace to throw the first blow.

"Pow!" The sound of Wallace's right fist went as it hit John's left hand because John had quickly raised his left arm to defend himself.

John took a step backward, hoping to reposition his legs for a counter swing at Wallace. As he did, he began losing his balance. Alertly noticing this, Serpenta saw an opportunity to position himself against John to cause him to fall. However, Natura, more alert than Serpenta, saw what he was going to do, and pushed Serpenta away from John. He then leaned against John's upper body to hold him upright. Natura didn't necessarily want to give John any advantage during the fight, but he surely didn't want John to be embarrassed by falling down either. Amazed at how he was able to keep his balance, John drew back his right arm with his fist balled up, ready for a strike.

"Kapow!" John's right fist caught Wallace's nose, squarely in the middle, enough to knock Wallace to the ground. Stunned by the blow, and certainly embarrassed as well, Wallace felt the pain and immediately felt blood run from his nose into this mouth as he breathed hard to catch his breath.

"Way to go, John Muir!" One of John's friends shouted. "Yes, way to go, John!" Another friend said.

Wallace's 'little gang of friends' didn't say a word. They just stared at Wallace, who was still trying to gain his composure and, of course, stop his nose from bleeding.

On his feet now, Wallace stuck out his right hand toward John. "Of course, I'm probably mistaken, John Muir! I can see that you are truly Scottish! I hope we can become good friends!"

John reached out and accepted Wallace's handshake. "I'm always friendly to everyone. I'm also ready to defend my Scottish honor, anytime, anyplace!"

John quickly improved his school ranking as a good fighter, but that improvement didn't mean that his fighting adventures were finished. There would be many other challenges from school mates who thought they were ready to take on the tall, scraggly John Muir. All of them found out they were not ready.

Like just about every other Scottish boy, John Muir had dreams of becoming a soldier. Many stories about the decades of wars between Scotland and England, and between Catholics and Protestants, had been learned in history classes and in each family's own historic experiences. Often times, Dunbar's 'soldier' boys would gather on a playground and reenact the battles their ancestors had fought. Not until much later in life did John become to realize that wars were not the answer for civilized people to live in peace.

# CHAPTER 8

## Climbing, Scrambling, and 'Scootching'

*"One of our best playgrounds was the famous old Dunbar Castle, to which King Edward fled after his defeat at Bannockburn. It was built more than a thousand years ago, and though we knew little of its history, we had heard many mysterious stories of the battles fought about its walls, and firmly believed that every bone we found in the ruins belonged to an ancient warrior. We tried to see who could climb highest on the crumbling peaks and crags, and took chances that no cautious mountaineer would try." John Muir (15)*

John's father forbade his children from playing outside the home with other children, who often wandered uncaringly across the countryside, sometimes in search of mischief. He feared that they might learn bad habits and language, get injured climbing over walls, or get caught by the game wardens for some violation. (16)

Every Saturday morning, before he left for work in his store, he said to his children, "You can play as much as you want in the back yard and walled garden, and mind that you don't disobey."

Even with this stern warning, knowing what a whipping he would certainly receive if caught, young John with several of his friends gathered at the north side of old Dunbar Castle early one Saturday morning. It was time to play one of their 'Castle Climbing

Games' as they called them. Stiff climbing competition it was! This morning's game was considered one of the toughest of all! Who would be the first to reach the top of the North Tower, the highest point of the castle, over two hundred feet high at low tide?

There was the usual chill in the air from the breezy North Sea. It was still low tide. The sea was naturally being pushed from the south, making it possible for the boys to walk along the base of the castle walls from Victoria Harbor to the North Tower. In a few hours, however, high tide would bring the high water once again, thereby making it impossible for them to easily walk back.

"Everyone knows the climbing rules," John said. "They're very simple. Be careful, don't look down, make sure you have a firm hand-hold on each rock, and support your climbing body with a good foot-hold. We have less than two hours to make the climb, return to the ground, and walk back to Victoria Harbor before high tide comes. Any questions?"

Natura looked at the faces of each boy and saw their worrisome looks as they gazed up at the rocky tower. But John's face didn't have a worried look at all. John's eyes had a wild, wandering look to them as he looked up. He then took several deep breaths and positioned his right leg for climbing.

"On your mark, get set, go!" John shouted.

With his right leg, John raised his slender body for the first step, quickly reset himself on his left leg and foot, reached for a hand-hold with his left hand, raised his body again, and soon got himself into a regular rhythm.

One of the boys, named Robert, soon started his climb. Not as experienced as John and the other boys, Robert was able to climb about twenty feet before he became too tired, or too scared, to climb anymore.

"I can't go anymore!" Robert said, alerting the other boys of his situation.

"That's alright, Robert," John replied, looking down at Robert and the other boys. "Just save enough strength to climb down. You'll do better next time! Be careful, that's the most important thing! And while you're waiting on us, keep a good eye on the tide. Give us a shout when high tide starts to come in."

John was very good at watching after his friends. He knew that they also looked after him.

William, another friend, also a very good climber, moved effortless it seemed, and stayed about even with John. But he knew that John would soon move well ahead of him.

"Oh, John, you have such a natural climbing rhythm!" William remarked. "Some grand day you'll be climbing the highest mountains, somewhere in this world."

Momentarily thinking about what William just said, the rock under John's left foot broke, leaving him hanging by his hands and right foot. He struggled to find another foot-hold for his left foot as he searched for another solid rock. Seeing John's situation, Natura quickly flew to just beneath him, placed his angelic energy behind John to hold him steady, and lifted him just enough for his left foot to find another rock. However, Serpenta was carefully watching as John lost his footing, thinking that John would surely fall before Natura could intervene. Even with Natura holding John up, Serpenta saw a brief opportunity to quickly fly near John's body, brush him with one of his wings, and cause him to fall. Upon seeing Serpenta make his move toward John, Natura simply thrust one of his large, strong wings out into Serpenta's flight path causing Serpenta to lose total control of his flight. With that, Serpenta spiraled down into the cold North Sea. Rising to the surface and catching his breath, he waved a wing at Natura and shouted, "I'll get you next time, Natura! You haven't seen the last of me!"

Natura paid little attention to Serpenta but quickly helped John regain his footing. John said, breathing very hard, "Whew, that was close! I didn't think I'd find a foot-hold so quickly."

William was looking in disbelief at John the whole time. "Well, John, as far I as could see, you didn't. Somehow, your body moved all at once to lift you up. Your guardian angel must truly be watching over you!"

"Could be, William. My good mother and grandmother believe in them, guardian angels that is."

John quickly resumed his climbing rhythm without giving his close-call any more thought. However, Natura breathed a sigh of relief, knowing that it was a matter of seconds before John completely lost his footing and balance, especially when Serpenta came so close to brushing John off the tower. Natura could have caught John in mid-air, but he didn't want John's rescue to be so unnatural- looking to his friends. He wanted to avoid causing an unusual spectacle that could be rumored to be a true 'miracle'.

Suddenly, Natura's angelic brain flashed forward to an image of he and John many years ahead, in the year 1872. One day in October of that year, John would find himself in a life or death situation as he climbed Mt. Ritter in California's Central Sierra Mountains. After reaching about 12,800 feet in elevation, he tried to climb a sheer wall of rock and ice to reach the summit, but soon found himself stuck, at a dead stop, with his arms spread wide, his body flat against the rock face, unable to move up or down. John thought his life would soon be over. He could envision a brief time of 'bewilderment' as he fell uncontrollably down the mountain face to the glacier frozen in time below. But before the dangerous vision was completed, he became wildly alert, his nerves becoming seriously shaken for the first time since climbing the mountain. Sensing his imminent death, John remembers suddenly becoming possessed by 'a new sense' which gained full control of his mind, body, and spirit. Years later, John would write in his own words what happened next: "The other self, bygone experiences, instinct, or Guardian Angel--call it what you will--came forward and assumed control. Then my trembling muscles became firm again, every rift and flaw in the rock was seen as through a microscope, and my limbs moved with a positiveness and precision with which I seemed to have nothing at all to do. Had I been borne aloft upon wings, my deliverance could not have been more complete." (17)

As Natura thought about this flash-forward vision, he said to himself, "Wow, I just hope I'll be ready to help John in that particularly instance by saving him from falling to a terrible death! I'm glad somehow that vision was given to me so I can train well to be ready to do my job."

Soon Natura's attention returned to the present moment as he observed John and the other two climbers continuing their climb of the North Tower.

The third climber, named Charles, was slowly climbing on the left side of William. Charles was more experienced than Robert but not as experienced as William and John. He was doing quite well as long as he gave close attention to his climbing. As such, he didn't look around at other climbers nor did he engage in conversation. While William and John stayed in close proximity to each other, Charles lagged considerably behind them.

The three climbing friends were now about forty-five minutes into their climb. John was about ten feet from the top, while William was about twenty feet from the top. Charles was about half way up the tower.

"High tide is a'coming in! High tide is a'coming in!" Robert shouted.

"Okay, Robert!" John acknowledged. "We'll have enough time to reach the top, catch our breath, and climb down. Don't worry!"

Reaching the very top of the tower now, John lifted himself into a standing position on a corner wall, breathed in a lung full of the cool, moist air, and said with quick, breathless words, "John Muir, a world-class mountain climber, reaches the summit of Mount North Tower!"

William soon joined him at the top.

"Welcome to the summit, William! Look at the view from up here!"

Choosing to sit rather than stand, William looked around to enjoy the sights from the tower's high vantage point. "Breathtaking! I can see the whole town and everything people are doing."

"And I can see all the way to the Fifth of Forth and count a dozen tall ships waiting for high tide to take their cargo to Edinburgh!" John replied. "It truly is a grand view! No mountaineer in Dunbar ever had a better view of God's boundless glory!" He waved both arms high over his head without a thought of falling.

"High tide is a'coming closer! You hear up there?!" Charles yelled with ever-increasing worry in his voice.

Hearing Robert, John looked down, and cupped his hands around his mouth. "Okay, Robert! We'll soon be on our way down!"

John looked down and over where Charles was resting about half way up the tower. "Charlie, good job! You made a good, honest climb today! We'll see you down below!"

The three mountaineers began their descent, which in many ways was more perilous than the upward climb. They would be unable to clearly see where to safety place their feet for a good, solid foot-hold. But they were experienced enough, and careful enough, to 'feel with their feet' the best places to position them.

Well within an hour and forty-five minutes from the start of their climb, and barely ahead of the incoming high tide, the three friends were soon standing on the narrow rock foundation that runs along the bottom of the tall tower. The North Sea waves were beginning to lap at their feet as high tide arose, like clockwork, in response to the natural attraction of the moon and the sun.

"Well done, mighty climbers!" John said, congratulating his friends. "Let's carefully but quickly make our way back to Victoria Harbor!"

Before they could safely reach the walls of the harbor, water was surrounding their ankles, making it difficult for them to see where to place their feet. Wet but safe now, they finally climbed over the harbor wall that separates the calm harbor from the turbulent North Sea.

Before they departed to go to their separate homes, John reminded them of next Saturday's excursion. "Don't forget that early next Saturday morning, we'll meet here to go on the most dangerous climb of all. During low tide, we'll play 'scootchers' by climbing down into the caverns running beneath the castle. Get here early, around six o'clock at the beginning of low tide."

During longer periods of low tide, they would play daring games that they called 'scootchers'. In these games at the old castle, the boys would dare each other to climb down into the deep dungeons located well below the dark water at high tide. Knowing that a crippling fall or a loss of direction would mean certain death when high tide returned, only the bravest made it all the way into the deeper dungeons. You might guess, John Muir was one of them. (18)

Later that day, after John and David were put to bed by their mother, John told David about the exciting climb he and his friends had made on the North Tower of Dunbar Castle. David was two years younger than John.

"Now David, when you become stronger and learn to climb, you can go with us to climb on the old castle. But you have to practice to become a good mountaineer. Let me show you."

John opened their bedroom window, went out onto the slate roof, and grabbed the window sill with both hands. He allowed his body to slip down and dangle in the wind for a minute or two. After a little rest back inside, he went out again and this time hung by one hand. Daring himself even further, he hung by one finger. Returning to the bedroom, he dared David to do the same.

"David, I dare you to try it! I'll be close enough to you to catch you if you fall. So, don't worry!"

David didn't want to be outdone by big brother John. He managed enough courage to crawl out the window, climb up to the top of the window-roof, and straddle it. But as he tried to return to the open window, he lost his courage. "I cannot get down! I cannot get down!"

"Don't cry, David. If you do, father will hear you and give both of us a terrible skelping."

Standing on the window sill and holding on by one hand to the window casing, John directed David. "David, slip your feet down to within my reach. After I have hold of your feet, I'll drag you inside the open window." David complied very nervously. John was inside and dragged David in by his heels. (19)

This ended mountaineer training and 'scootching' for the night. Both John and David gladly went to bed, although they were very frightened by this whole 'scootcher' adventure. Nevertheless, Natura was present with both John and David the entire time. He was ready to help both boys at any time.

# CHAPTER 9

## The Beginnings of Lifelong Wanderings

*"Our amusements on Saturday afternoons and vacations depended mostly on getting away from home into the country, especially in the spring when the birds were calling loudest...We stole away to the seashore or the green, sunny fields with almost religious regularity, taking advantage of opportunities, when father was very busy, to join our companions, oftenest to hear the birds sing and hunt their nests, glorying in the number we had discovered and called our own...It was far too common a practice among us to carry off a young lark just before it could fly, place it in a cage, and fondly, laboriously feed it. Sometimes we succeeded in keeping one alive for a year or two...At last, conscience-stricken, we carried the beloved prisoner to the meadow west of Dunbar where it was born, and, blessing its sweet heart, bravely set it free, and our exceeding great reward was to see it fly and sing in the sky." John Muir (20)*

"Wake up, David!" John said as he shook David, lying next to him in bed. "Father's busy working in the store by now. I told Willie Chisholm and Bob Richardson I'd meet them south of Belhaven Bay to look for birds near Caravan Park. You want to go with us?"

"I guess, John, but I'm scared Father will discover we've gone and give us a good whooping when we get home! Maybe I can just stay home and cover for you in case Papa asks about your whereabouts."

"Yes, you could, but I need your help in getting over the garden's rock wall. Come on, David, we'll have some fun seeing all the different birds and finding a few of their nests!"

"Well, okay."

The two boys quickly dressed and went down the stairs to the kitchen to eat breakfast. On the kitchen table was a note from their mom. John picked it up and read it aloud so David would hear. "My dear children, I'm across the street helping Grandmother Gilrye clean some fish she bought at the harbor market this morning. Your oatmeal porridge is in the cooling box with the milk. Eat a good breakfast and play in the backyard garden until I get home, probably in a few hours. Love, Mom".

"Well, that's a stroke of good luck, David. That'll give us plenty of time to wander in the woods, count some birds, and find a few of their nests. Let's hurry and eat our breakfast!"

Breakfast was quickly eaten. John and David ran into the backyard garden and stopped near the back wall nearest the street, the one that leads to Belhaven Bay Caravan Park.

"Now, David, get on your hands and knees, stiffen your back, and pretend you're a step-stool. I'll gently step on you so I can reach the top of the wall. Once I'm up on the top, I'll hang by my one arm, reach down, and pull you up with the other arm. Okay?"

"Okay!"

Natura, always present with John, stood very close to them next to the wall. He floated himself in the air just enough to be over John as his tall body stretched upward to climb over the tall garden wall. He said to himself, *"Don't worry, John, I'm here to help lift you, or catch you if you should fall!"*

John gently stepped onto David's back, reached just enough to place both hands on the wall's top, and slowly lifted himself up. He hung his left leg over the wall and reached down with his right hand. David grabbed his hand and arm tightly with both hands. John lifted him to the top of the wall. Catching his breath, John swung himself around to the other side of the wall.

"Now, David, we'll do the same thing on this side. Hold on tightly to my hand and I'll lower you down to the ground."

Once again, Natura floated in the air next to them, ready to assist if either needed help.

Once John and David were safely on the ground, they walked briskly down Belhaven Road toward the Belhaven Bay Caravan Park. Traffic was heavy at this early hour because many farmers were traveling into town with their wagons filled with fresh vegetables and fruits to sell at Dunbar's farmers' market. Other people were also traveling into town to buy the farmers' fresh produce at the market located near the harbors. And, most everyone would buy some fresh fish from the fishermen who'd just arrived at the harbor with their morning catch.

"Wait up Johnnie!" A voice from behind John and David shouted.

Turning around, they saw Willie Chisholm and Bob Richardson strolling toward them. "I thought you said you'd meet us at the park!" John said as the two stragglers caught up with he and David.

"I did, but my mom wouldn't let me leave the house until I'd cleaned my room!" Willie replied.

"Well, I was just waiting on Willie to come by my house," Bob said, as if he couldn't find a better excuse.

Soon the four boys were walking through the Belhaven Bay Caravan Park with its glorious natural beauty. It was a very large park filled with many varieties of trees, plants, flowers, and, of course, hundreds of birds. Located near a wide meadow, many birds flew between the open fields and the woods in search of food and shelter.

"Hey, John, let's have a bird counting contest! Here're the rules. Write the names of each different bird you see in a notebook. Whoever counts the most different types of birds wins! Okay?" Willie said.

"Okay, Willie. David will come with me and Bob will go with you. That seems fair enough."

The two pairs headed in opposite directions. Willie and Bob headed toward a large field just opposite the park's woods. John and David walked toward the woods.

John pulled a small notebook and a pencil from his pants-pocket to be ready to write the birds' names and make a tally mark for each bird he and David saw. They would also look for a few bird nests just for fun.

"Now, David, just let me know when you see a bird, any kind, so I can see it, identify it, and write it in my notebook. I know you can't name the birds very well, but I'll tell you what they are so you can begin learning."

"Okay, John, I see a bird behind you!" David pointed to a yellow-bellied bird in an apple tree.

Turning around quickly, John spotted the bird. Sure enough, it had a yellow-looking belly and was pecking at a large apple in an apple tree. John took out his little hand telescope, placed it to his right eye, and looked more carefully at the bird. He noted its sharp pointed bill, the red coloring on its throat and its forehead, large white wing patches, a white rump, and that it was eating an apple. John had seen a few of these birds before and at first thought they were woodpeckers. After he looked it up in his bird guide book, he discovered it was a yellow-bellied sapsucker, which belongs to the woodpecker family but has a different name. (21)

"One yellow-bellied sapsucker, David!" John wrote in his little notebook. "Good job, David!"

"Wow!" David was excited that he'd found their first bird to count.

"Well, David, this is a good time for me to teach you a few things about birds. Would you like to know about them?"

"I would! I would, John!"

"Very well, let's sit on this fallen tree." John opened his bird guide book to a section about how to identify birds. They both climbed on top of the fallen tree and sat down. David looked down at the page as John pointed to the first important criteria about bird identification.

"David, first look at the bird's size. As a good rule of thumb, use the size of other familiar birds for comparison. For example, is it smaller than a black bird or larger than a common sparrow? Answering this question will help provide the first clue about any bird's identification. Next, look at the bird's body shape. Is it plump like a starling or slender like an oriole? Then, study the shape of its wings. Are they rounded like a woodpecker's or sharply pointed like a dove? Similarly, look at the shape of its tail. Is it rounded like a blue jay's or pointed like a mourning dove? And what's the shape of its bill? Birds with stout and short bills, like sparrows, use them to crack seeds. Birds of prey usually have hook-tipped bills for attacking and eating their prey." (22)

For each identification criteria, John would turn to the pages to show David a drawing of each bird so he could actually see the differences. "Wow, John, there are lots of things to know about birds!" David looked down at the bird guide book.

"Sure are, David, but this is only the beginning of what to look for in each bird."

John turned the page of the bird guide book, ran a finger down the page, and stopped in the middle. "This is also a very important factor. Look at how the bird behaves. Does it cock its tail like a wren or hold it down like a flycatcher? Does it climb trees like a woodpecker using its tail as a brace? Or does it climb down headfirst like a nuthatch? How does it fly? Does it glide or soar like a hawk, dip up and down like a flicker, or fast and straight like a dove? Observing its behavior will give you many more clues about the bird. And finally, look at the bird's markings and patterns on its head, body, wings, tail, and rump." (23)

"Whew, John, how can I remember all of those things?" David was overwhelmed with all the information details about bird identification.

"Well, David, the best way to learn is to practice watching birds a lot. Now there seem to be more birds flying around in the woods. I expect Willie and Bob are in the nearby fields watching for birds to count, and they've caused the birds to fly into the woods where we are. So, let's start practicing some of the things I showed you in the bird guide book."

Many different birds were flying in all directions as John and David slowly sauntered along, looking very carefully as a bird would land on a nearby tree limb and stay long enough for them to study its features. David was more excited than ever to help John identify the different birds! John's short lesson about how to identify birds had certainly bolstered his self-confidence, although he could only identify a few birds correctly. At least he was trying very hard.

"There's a bluebird, John!" David pointed to a bird in the tree just above them.

"You're right, David. It is blue in color, but let's look closer at it to see what kind of bird it is. It could be a blue jay, a true bluebird, a blue grosbeak, or some other bird with blue feathers."

John opened his bird guide book. David stood next to him so he could also see the book. "Remember, David, what we learned in our first lesson about birds a while ago." John slowly ran his finger down a page which summarized some of the identification information.

"Oh, yes, John," David looked first at the information on the page and then looked at the bird in the tree just above them. "It's not a very large bird. I'd say it's about the size of a sparrow. Its body is sort of round and plump, and not very slender. It has regular looking tail feathers and has no markings on its wings." (24)

As both John and David looked at the bird, John began turning the pages of the bird guide book, stopping at each page that had a blue-colored bird on it. "There, John, I think it's a true bluebird!" David placed a finger on the page showing several different kinds of bluebirds.

"Well, David, I think you're correct. If you look closely at the bluebird's head, you'll also see that its head feathers are smoothly rounded and don't project out toward it's back like those of the blue jay." (24) John flipped the pages from the bluebird to the blue jay. As he did, David said, "You're right, John!"

"Well done, David! Now, let me record the bluebird in my notebook."

There were so many different birds landing in nearby trees that John and David had no trouble identifying many birds. To help out, Natura would place his angelic wings around each bird to keep it from flying away. By his doing this, John and David had plenty of time to observe each bird, compare its features with the bird guide book, and correctly identify it. Just to be sure they'd win the contest with Willie and Bob, they recorded a dozen different birds in John's little notebook.

"That should do it, David. We now have identified twelve different birds. Let's walk back to the pathway between the woods and the large field to meet Willie and Bob. By now, they should be finished with their count."

John and David followed a well-marked trail leading from the woods to the meeting place. Natura was hovering just over their heads, as always, to guide and protect John.

After walking for about ten minutes, John and David arrived at the meeting place, but Willie and Bob were not there. John and David decided to walk toward the field where they thought Willie and Bob were still counting birds. Sure enough, they saw their two friends in the middle of the field that overlooks a large meadow.

When Willie and Bob saw John and David approaching the field, Bob slowly walked to meet them. Willie stayed behind to write the names of the birds in a small notebook, just as John had done. Finally finished, he caught up with Bob and the two of them met up with John and David.

"Well, how many different birds did you two count?" Willie asked.

"We counted a dozen!" David said excitedly.

"So, did we!" Bob replied.

"Well, go ahead and name the birds you counted," John said.

"Let's see now." Willie removed his notebook from his shirt pocket, flipped a few pages, and looked carefully at his notes. "We've got a chickadee, nuthatch, finch, sparrow, cardinal, junco, bunting, blue jay, mockingbird, thrasher, blackbird, and oriole. I do believe that's twelve different types of birds."

"What birds did you count?" Bob asked.

John removed his notebook from his pants-pocket and opened it. "We've got a yellow-bellied sapsucker, bluebird, sparrow, blue jay, cardinal, woodpecker, nuthatch, titmouse, red crossbill, purple finch, wren, and mockingbird."

"We have to do something to break the tie!" Willie said, in disbelief that indeed they were tied in the bird-counting contest.

"What can we do?" David asked.

Natura thought about it for a moment. He had an idea! He'd seen several skylarks nesting in the tall grass several yards from the four boys. He thought if he disturbed them enough by flapping his wings near them, they'd start flying. The boys could then play one of their favorite games of watching the birds soar high into the sky until they couldn't see them any longer. And so, he hovered right next to their nesting area and flapped his large angelic wings.

Suddenly a male skylark sprang from the tall grass only a stone's throw away from the four boys! As it began soaring high into the sky, it began singing wonderful songs that only skylarks can sing. Soaring higher, it sang a long, sweet song as it effortlessly shot straight up to a height of over forty feet. As the young skylark was almost out of sight, another male skylark sprang up from the same spot to follow his friend into the sky.

"I know what we can do to break the tie!" John said. "We can watch the second skylark soar into the sky. Whoever can see him last before he's out of sight will be the winner. Are you agreeable to this tiebreak idea?" (26)

Willie and Bob looked at each other. They knew John had thrown down a good challenge. And they didn't have a better idea for breaking the tie.

Nodding to one another in agreement, Willie turned to John. "Yes, we agree!"

The four boys quickly looked at the second skylark as it started soaring, straight up, just like the first one had done. It also began to sing a beautiful skylark melody.

"I see him!" Willie said.

"I see him too!" Bob then said.

John and David also shouted that they could see him.

Going higher, higher while continuing to sing its sweet song, it's powerful wings quickly moved it nearly beyond sight.

"I see him yet!" Willie shouted.

"Me too!" Bob said.

"I don't see him anymore!" David said, rather disappointedly. "Do you John?"

"Yes, I see him clearly!"

"I see him yet!" Willie said again.

"I don't see him!" Bob said.

"I can still see him, and also hear him!" John shouted.

Not seeing him anymore, Willie didn't want to admit defeat. So, he said, "I think I see him!"

"What do you mean, Willie?" John said. "You either see him or not! I can still see him! Can you see him or not, Willie? Just be honest about it!"

"Okay, I guess I can't see him now."

Not to rub it in that he and David had won the contest, John simply said, "We have to get home before our father knows we're gone."

"We'll walk with you," Bob said.

The four boys walked down a path that led to Belhaven Road. It was now around ten o'clock in the morning. The traffic of people going into Dunbar was still pretty heavy. The four friends soon reached the town limits, passed the grammar school and the primary school, and arrived at the corner of High Street.

"We'll see you boys next time," John said, as he and David ran toward their house on High Street. Bob and Willie went in the opposite direction toward their houses.

Once again, John and David helped each other over their backyard garden's rock wall. As usual, Natura hovered very close to them to make sure they didn't fall. Once over the wall and on the ground, they walked quickly but quietly to the kitchen door. Carefully opening it, they peeked inside to see if their mother had returned from Grandmother Gilrye's. Seeing that she hadn't returned, they knew they were safe.

Natura thought about the habit John and David were developing in disobeying their father and mother. He knew that he had to provide some guidance to help them break this habit. He suddenly saw an opportunity. Looking through the wall into the large storage room where Daniel stored his supplies, he saw Daniel loading several large bags of oats onto a dolly. Seeing some gardening tools resting against the outside wall on the porch, Natura pushed them to the floor where they made a loud clanking sound, enough to be heard by Daniel inside the storage room.

"*What was that?" he thought. "Just the boys dropping some garden tools onto the floor?*" He decided to check on the sound, *and* on the boys. He quickly opened the door to the kitchen to find John and David standing there with a surprised look on their faces.

"What are you doing boys? Working in the garden? I heard some garden tools falling to the porch floor." Daniel looked out the kitchen's screen door to see the tools scattered on the floor. "Yes, there they are. Don't you boys know how to properly put them away after using them?" He looked intently at John and David for their reply.

John and David looked at their father, then looked questioningly toward each other, as if asking, "*What should we say?*"

"No, Papa, we weren't working in the garden," John said.

Then David blurted out the truth because he couldn't hold it in any longer. "We were out with our friends, Bob and Willie, at Belhaven Bay Caravan Park counting birds."

"Well, I hope you counted a lot of birds, enough to last for a long time because it'll be a long time before you go bird watching again! I know Bob and Willie are good boys, and that bird-counting is not a bad thing to do. Nevertheless, you've disobeyed me and your mother. You know we forbade you to leave the house and the garden walls without our permission. Right?"

"Yes, sir, Papa!" John and David replied in unison. Their heads hung sadly against their chests.

"Here are the consequences for your disobedience. Tonight, after supper, you'll tell the whole family what you've done. I'll whip you on the buttocks with my switch and send you to bed. You'll not be allowed out of the house or yard for two weeks, unless you're accompanied by either your mother or myself. I think that's fair enough. Understand boys?"

"Yes, sir, Papa!" Both boys said in union.

"Now, go fetch a fresh bucket of water for my customers and place it on the main store counter, please!"

John and David fetched a bucket of water from the well, placed it on the main store counter, and returned to the back yard to play, and to think about the whipping they'd receive later.

They also thought about their bird-counting excursion. They had enjoyed another day of wildness, slipping away from home, seeing so much of nature's wonderful attractions, and competing with friends in the counting of endless birds. For now, it seemed that the wonderful adventure might be worth the consequences.

# CHAPTER 10

## Tales of America and A New World

*"No more grammar, but boundless woods full of mysterious good things; trees full of sugar, growing in ground full of gold; hawks, eagles, pigeons, filling the sky; millions of birds' nests, and no gamekeepers to stop us in all the wild, happy land. We were utterly, blindly glorious." John Muir (27)*

While in grammar school, John was introduced to his first natural history images of America, which was sometimes referred to as 'The New World' by some students. In one of their reading books, 'Maccoulough's Course of Reading', John's natural imagination was stimulated by natural history sketches along with vivid descriptions of such predators as America's bald eagles and fish hawks. John was also excited, as well as saddened, by Audubon's moving story of America's passenger pigeons which assembled in such large flocks that they appeared as large dark clouds in the sky. (28) However, over time, the pigeons were soon annihilated by farmers who thoughtlessly killed them in mass and fed them to their farm animals. (29) It was a beginning lesson in the need to preserve nature's delicate balance that remained with John all his life.

John also learned about some of America's vast forests and their great variety of many different trees. He and his friends particularly thought that the sugar maple was a most interesting tree because of its natural ability to produce delicious sweet maple syrup. And like the rest of the world, everybody in Scotland was talking about the discovery of gold in America's farthest western state, California. (29) But John would never have guessed that he and his family would become one of the many Scottish families to actually move to America!

"Well, boys, you don't need to learn your lessons for tonight because we're going to America in the morning!" Daniel said as John and David sat around Grandfather Gilrye's fireplace one night learning their school lessons.

"Oh, Papa, are you just joking with us?" John asked.

Looking at the seriousness of his father's face, he knew he wasn't joking.

"No, my Johnnie boy, I'm not joking. Every Scotchman nowadays dreams of a better life for his family. The new world of America offers us that great opportunity! We'll have lots of land, a good house, and a democratic government under which we can be people of true freedom. And I have to say, my boy, my heart is restless to save souls for Jesus Christ. In America, we can freely share our brand of Christianity with many people who're hungry for the truth!"

John and David jumped to their feet and began to dance a Scottish jig. They laughed and chatted excitedly about their father's good news. But they hardly noticed the saddened faces of Grandmother and Grandfather Gilrye as they tried to absorb this heart-rending news and what it would mean to be without their dear family just across the street. They only knew that their lives would be very empty and sad as they lived out their old age without their young family.

After Daniel left the house, Grandfather Gilrye crossed the large parlor room and sat down in a chair next to John and David. "My dear grandboys, I want to give you each a gold coin as a keepsake." He handed each boy a gold coin. "Someday, you can use it to buy something special and remember your good grandparents who dearly love you. We'll surely miss you very much."

Grandmother Gilrye came over to the boys. She took the boys under each of her arms. Saying nothing, just hugging each boy tightly, she stared blankly into the dark space beyond the light of the fireplace.

Grandfather Gilrye then said, "I know you're excited about America, and the many wonderful new things to enjoy. You certainly should be. But my dear laddies, you'll also find plenty of hard work as you clear the land, build your new house, plant your crops, and harvest them. You both will have to grow up very quickly to become strong young men. God bless you both!"

Natura observed and listened very carefully because this huge change in John and his family's home location would also mean many changes for him. He would, of course, have to watch over John as he traveled to America by way of a train, a sailing ship, a river boat, a canal boat, a lake steamer, and a horse-drawn wagon. Natura thought, "*Whatever ways the Muirs traveled and wherever they ended up living, I'll have to learn many new things in order to continue protecting and guiding John.*"

Sleep for the Muir family hardly came at all the night of February 18, 1849. Daniel and three of his children, John, David, and Sarah, were busy packing their clothes, books, personal things, and everything else they could manage to fit into their large footlocker-type luggage and wooden boxes. The other family members, Anne, Margaret, Danny, Mary, and Anna would stay behind in Scotland and travel to America once a suitable home was ready. But they didn't know how long that would be.

Daniel, of course, had to pack pots and pans for cooking, other household items to use in their new home, tools for building a house and farming the virgin land, and food for their trans-Atlantic journey. Like many others who were immigrating to America, he probably packed too much! In one large box alone, he packed an old-fashioned scale with its complete set of cast iron counterweights. Two of the counterweights weighed fifty-six pounds each, two twenty-eights pounds each, and downward until the lowest weighed one pound. The entire box probably weighed near four hundred pounds.

Early on the morning of February 19, 1849, the Muir family, Grandfather and Grandmother Gilrye, and several close friends gathered at the Dunbar railway station. As the train bound for the port of Glasgow arrived, much excitement could be observed on the train platform as other departing family members said their farewells. In some cases, a few family members would never see their departing family members again. This was the case for Grandmother and Grandfather Gilrye. They would never see their son-in-law, Daniel, and their grandchildren, John, David, and Sarah, again. And it would be a long time before the rest of the family saw them again.

"We will miss you children ever so much!" Grandmother Gilrye said as she hugged John, David, and Sarah tightly against her. Grandfather Gilrye now joined her in embracing the children.

"And oh, how we'll miss you, Grammy and Grandpa!" John said. He was trying not to cry, but he did anyway. David and Sarah were also crying as they hugged their grandparents for the last time.

Daniel embraced Anne and kissed her lightly on the cheek. "Goodbye, my dear, take good care of yourself and the children, as well as your mother and father! May all of God's blessings be with you!"

"And you four," speaking to Margaret, Danny, Mary, and Anna, "take good care of yourselves, your mother, and your grandparents!" He hugged them tightly and gave them each a kiss.

Finally, Daniel, embraced his in-laws, David and Margaret Gilrye. "Goodbye and God bless both of you! We'll surely miss you! Please take good care of yourselves as well as Anne and the children!"

"We will, son! And God's blessings to you always!"

It was time for the train to depart Dunbar for Glasgow. There the four would board an old-fashioned sailing ship to cross the great Atlantic Ocean to America. Once the old ship left the Scottish port of Glasgow, it would take over six weeks for it to cross the Atlantic.

On the very first day at sea, the four Muirs worked together to build a shelter for the cooking stove, food provisions, and kitchen supplies. Sarah boldly took charge of preparing their first breakfast, but her cooking endeavors only lasted a short time. She soon succumbed to the dreadful seasickness and stayed below deck in bed for most of the long voyage. Daniel soon fell ill with nausea and took to his bunk for comfort. John and David remained well and wildly played on the open deck with other children their age. They also hung around the sailors while they worked and eagerly hoped to help them.

John said to David, "Let's go watch the sailors do their rope-hauling and climbing work. Maybe they'll need our help!" The sailors often let the boys help with the ropes; they even taught them the names of different ropes and sails. However, they would not allow the boys to climb the ropes to unfurl the sails or to secure them during fierce storms. Nevertheless, John and David wanted to because they thought they were good enough climbers.

"Storms a'coming in! Storms a'coming! All hands secure the main sails!" The captain shouted on his old-fashioned megaphone. All the sailors heard the captain's orders. John and David also heard.

While John and David watched the sailors scurry up the ropes, they thought and wondered how they could help. Watching very carefully, they saw each sailor climb flawlessly and fearlessly crawl along the mast arms to tie the sails as each was hoisted by the deck hands. "Look David, one of the sailors on the short mast pole seems to be stuck! His foot is caught in a small rope!"

"Yes, John. I can see him! What can we do to help?"

"He's not that high up. I'll climb up to where his foot is stuck and help unstick it! You can stay on deck and watch for me. Find another sailor nearby and let them know what's happening!"

"Okay, John!"

John started climbing up the short mast post. He was used to climbing most everything but was not used to climbing poles, especially with gusty winds blowing him around so fiercely. Getting near the sailor whose foot was caught in a small rope, John reached to dislodge the foot. As he did, he lost his balance. His right foot slipped from one of the mast's ladder arms. As it did, it caught a small mast rope and became entangled, similar to what had happened to the sailor's foot.

While trying to keep an eye on John, David also looked around for a sailor who he could ask to help. Natura also was keeping his eyes on John. So was Serpenta. Which one would get to John first? Serpenta quickly saw an opportunity to cause John to fall from the mast pole. He would only have to push John's body enough to cause his left foot to slip from the mast's ladder arm. John would surely fall to his death to the deck or be blown overboard into the turbulent Atlantic Ocean. Aiming for John's body, Serpenta flew like the wind! But not faster than Natura! Natura immediately saw what Serpenta was trying to do. He instantly flew to John's body, wrapped his large wings around him, and blocked Serpenta as he made contact with him, John, and the mast post. Unable to regain control of his body, Serpenta tumbled to the deck with a 'thud'.

"What was that?" A sailor said as he turned to investigate. Of course, he didn't see the invisible Serpenta lying helplessly on the deck but he did hear David calling him. Then he saw him. Running toward David, the sailor saw him pointing up at the mast pole. He then saw one of the sailors caught in the ropes, and also John hanging precariously just below him. However, John was not hanging but was resting in Natura's secure wings, unseen by any humans standing on the deck. The sailor patted David on the back. "Don't worry, son, we'll get them both down from those ropes safely!"

As Natura held securely onto John, he waited for the sailor to climb the mast pole. As he neared John's location, Natura gently swung John over to him. Now in the sailor's arm, Natura stayed close to John as the sailor climbed safely down to the deck. By this time, another sailor started climbing up the mast pole to the sailor caught in the ropes. With just a little support and help, the sailor removed his foot from the rope and carefully climbed down to the deck's safety.

With all the main sails now safely secured, along with the sailor and John safely on deck, the whole gang of sailors danced around with joyful songs of celebration. Although each person was wet, cold, and tired, they all sang as if the sun was shining brightly on a calm summer day.

After a few days in his bunk, Daniel recovered enough to climb the stairs to the main deck. Seeing him weakly walk to the railing on the lee side of the ship, John and David ran over to greet him.

"Well, my laddies, I see you both are doing well," Daniel said, looking more nauseated as he tried to adjust to the rocking and reeling of the old ship. "Good for you."

"We sure are, Papa!" John replied. David nodded his head dramatically, showing his agreement with John.

"Well, as you see, your sister and I are having a bad spell of seasickness. You'll have to fend for yourselves in preparing whatever meals you're able to do."

"Don't worry, Papa," David said. "Out kindly neighbors have been helping us out by inviting us to their meals."

"Papa, do you know where we will settle in the New World?" John asked.

"I first thought we'd settle in Canada but I've learned that it's so densely wooded that it'd take a lifetime to clear enough trees for farming. Keeping my ears open, I've heard that America's state of Wisconsin has good fertile land and not as many woods to clear. I'm especially interested in southeastern Wisconsin where there's much news about a canal being planned to join the Fox and Wisconsin Rivers. Once that happens, there'll be one waterway for boats to travel from the St. Lawrence River to the Gulf of Mexico. This will make it very convenient for the local famers to ship their grains to both Canada and the Southern United States."

"That Wisconsin state seems like a good choice for settlement to me, Papa," John said. "I would think the vast virgin land there would have an abundance of birds, wild animals, fish, and lots of beautiful trees and wild flowers!"

"I'm sure it does, Johnnie, but first we've got to build a suitable house, clear the land, and plant our crops before you boys can wander too far to enjoy those natural things."

John and David were hardly listening as much as they were thinking about all the wildness their new homeland would have. But before they arrived there, there was a lot of wildness to enjoy around the old ship as they watched for whales, dolphins, porpoises, and seabirds. Leaving their father holding on tightly to the ship's railing, still looking very sick, the boys ran lengthwise to the front of the ship to enjoy their 'watching'. Natura was right behind them, as always.

Finally, the long, long voyage was nearing its end. Well, almost. They still had a lot of miles to travel through a number of America's rivers, canals, and Great Lakes. After a brief stop at the New York City harbor, Daniel and the children boarded a smaller boat that carried them up the Hudson River to Albany, New York. At Albany, they boarded an Erie Canal packet boat, a boat that carries passengers, freight, and mail. As they journeyed up the Hudson River and then through connecting canals to Buffalo, New York, they enjoyed seeing their first American towns as the boats stopped to unload and load passengers as well as freight and mail. Finally arriving at Buffalo, which is located on Lake Erie, they boarded a lake steamer that took them across the Great Lakes of Erie, Huron, and Michigan to their port destination of Milwaukee, Wisconsin.

# CHAPTER 11

## Wisconsin's Glorious Marquette County!

*"This sudden plash into pure wildness--baptism in Nature's warm heart--how utterly happy it made us! Nature streaming into us, wooingly teaching her wonderful glowing lessons, so unlike the dismal grammar ashes and cinders so long thrashed into us. Here without knowing it we still were at school; every wild lesson a love lesson, not whipped but charmed into us. Oh, that glorious Wisconsin wilderness! Everything new and pure in the very prime of the spring when Nature's pulses were beating highest and mysteriously keeping time with our own! Young hearts, young leaves, flowers, animals, the winds and the streams and the sparkling lake, all widely, gladly rejoicing together!" John Muir (30)*

The Milwaukee port was very busy. Several ships were docked at the pier to unload their passengers and cargo, and then to reload as they prepared to sail to other ports in America or to other places around the world. Daniel and the three children gathered their personal belongings and walked down the gangplank. Many people crowded the pier, either disembarking from one of the half dozen ships at the pier, or preparing to board one of them to begin their sailing journey.

"Now, Sarah, John, and David, stay together at this street corner and watch our belongings while I locate someone with a wagon to take us to Kingston, Wisconsin," Daniel said to his children.

Daniel walked toward a busy market place a few blocks away where he hoped to hire someone with a large wagon. When he got to the bustling market area, he looked carefully at either the wagons being unloaded or the empty wagons whose owners were hoping to take a load on their return home.

"*There's one*!" Daniel thought to himself as he spotted a large empty wagon with its owner standing next to it. He walked up the owner. "Sir, my family and I need transportation to Kingston, Wisconsin, for ourselves and our belongings. Could we hire you to take us there?"

"Well, you sure can! As a matter of fact, I live only ten miles from Kingston. I just finished unloading a load of wheat from my farm and was hoping to find a load to haul back my way. You're in luck, Mister! I mean, we're both in luck!"

"The bulk of my belongings are now being unloaded onto the dock. And my three children are waiting with our personal belongings at the street corner a few blocks down that way." Daniel said as he pointed down the street where he'd left the children.

"What will you charge to take us and our belongings to Kingston?"

Stroking his long beard, the Marquette County farmer took very little time to think about a price because he already knew what he'd charge. "I think thirty dollars is a fair price."

"You've got a deal!" Daniel replied.

Both the farmer and Daniel were very happy to make a deal. Daniel was especially happy and so were the children when Daniel returned to tell them. It took a good while to load the large number of belongings they'd brought from Scotland, which now included a cast-iron cooking stove Daniel bought at Buffalo. There was barely enough room for Daniel and the children to sit or ride on the crowded, over-loaded wagon. Natura had no problem at all; he simply floated just over the top of the wagon and its heavy load.

The hundred-mile trip from Milwaukee to Kingston was extremely difficult, to say the least, as the heavy-laden wagon, pulled by four large horses, trudged wearily over newly thawed roadways filled with heavy mud and deep ruts. After many times of the wagon getting stuck, the farmer wished he'd never agreed to take the load. Each time the wagon got stuck, everyone jumped off the wagon and helped push it through the deep, muddy ruts. Natura also helped. He placed his large angelic body against the back of the wagon and thrust his energy field forward as much as he could. Serpenta just floated around observing the agonizing, muddy activity, and caring less about anyone but himself.

After a week of traveling, Daniel Muir and his children finally arrived at Kingston. Daniel rented a room at the Kingston Inn where he left the children while he traveled several miles into Marquette County to find a farmer named Alexander Gray. A land-agent at Kingston gave Daniel his name, telling him Mr. Gray would probably help him find some good farming land.

Within an hour after Daniel left Kingston, John and David were out and about playing with some of the boys in the little town. It took them no time at all to feel right at home! Sarah rested in their room at the Inn. She was still very exhausted and weary from the very long journey from Scotland, and, of course, she thought she'd never get over the many days of seasickness on the old sailing ship.

In a few days, Daniel returned to Kingston.

"Children, get your personal belongings packed and get ready to leave," Daniel announced as he opened the door to the rented room. "I've found us some good farming land next to a fine wooded area overlooking a beautiful, spring-fed lake. Mr. Alexander Gray is coming with his large wagon and a team of three yoke of oxen to haul us to our new homeland."

"Oh, happy day, Papa!" John shouted as he leaped to his feet.

"Yes, Papa, I can't wait to see our new farm land!" David said while grabbing a few clothes to pack into his foot-locker luggage.

"I'm just happy to be on dry land and not reeling on that old crate of a ship!" Sarah said.

Within a short time, Mr. Gray pulled up in front of the Inn with a large wagon pulled by three yokes of oxen. The Muir's belongings were stored on the Inn's front porch. Mr. Gray and Daniel began to load the wagon. They grunted from time to time as they worked together to lift the heavy stove and many wooden crates filled with household supplies, farming tools, and, of course, the unusually heavy crate filled with four hundred pounds of weights. A few of the local citizens also stopped and took time to help them load. During these early frontier days, everybody jumped in to help anyone needing help. It was simply one of the most important 'Golden Rules' everyone followed no matter from what country they came.

Before leaving town, Daniel looked around to find a pony for sale. He'd promised the children before they left Scotland that he'd get them one once they settled down in America. Soon he found and bought a little Indian pony for thirteen dollars from a storekeeper who'd recently bought it from an Indian. The little pony, now named Jack, was securely tied to the back of the wagon to the great excitement of John and David.

Once the wagon was loaded, Mr. Gray guided the white oxen as they pulled the heavy load out of Kingston. The ten-mile ride over a narrow, primitive road was enjoyable for the children, especially when they rode in, out, and around wooded areas richly filled with nature's finest trees, plants, wild flowers, and animal critters.

As the large oxen pulled the heavy wagon with chains harnessed to their muscular front shoulders to crooked pieces of yokes hung over their necks, John thought to himself, *"How do such large, docile animals move so gracefully from right to left around trees and stumps when the farmer commands them with only 'haw' and 'gee'?*

Upon arriving at Mr. Gray's house, Daniel left the children once again for a few days while he and Mr. Gray went to the Muir's future home site. "Now, children, Mr. Gray and I are going to our farm to build a shanty. I expect you to help Mrs. Gray with the chores and to be good children. And Sarah, Mrs. Gray is going to give you lessons in how to cook on a kitchen stove."

"Yes, Papa," Sarah nodded. John and David also nodded, but quietly looked toward the nearby woods, and also at the freshly planted fields Mr. Gray had cultivated from the natural wilderness. As John and David looked at the fields, they had no idea of the hard, hard work they would face when they would help their father prepare their virgin land for the planting of wheat, corn, hay, and a variety of vegetables. At this moment, their hearts were set on exploring Mr. Gray's wild property for birds and every natural critter imaginable!

As soon as Mr. Gray and Daniel were out of sight, John and David ran wildly into the fields, meadows, and woods to begin their first 'wanderings' of all things natural in their new country called America. They ran, jumped, and laughed with endless joy! With so much to see and do, they barely stopped long enough to look closely at the trees, plants, flowers, birds, snakes, squirrels, beavers, and turtles, among many wonderful natural things. They just knew they'd have endless days to see and enjoy everything, time and time again.

*"Whew!"* Natura thought to himself, *"I've got my hands full keeping up with these two boys!"* But he did a good job protecting them from any danger, and he was always watchful for any of Satan's evil spirits who continued to look for opportunities to harm the boys.

With the help of many good neighbors, Mr. Gray and Daniel built the little shanty in about a day, using rough logs cut from nearby trees and lumber purchased from a local saw miller. They also used the square nails stored in several wooden kegs that Daniel had brought from Scotland.

# CHAPTER 12

## A Little Shanty and Freedom to Wander

*"To this charming hut, in the sunny woods, overlooking a flowery glacier meadow and a lake rimmed with white water lilies, we were hauled by an ox-team across trackless carex swamps and low rolling hills sparsely dotted with round-headed oaks. Just as we arrived at the shanty, before we had time to look at it or the scenery about it, David and I jumped down in a hurry off the load of household goods, for we had discovered a blue jay's nest, and in a minute or so we were up the tree beside it, feasting our eyes on the beautiful green eggs and beautiful birds--our first memorable discovery...Then we ran along the brow of the hill that the shanty stood on, and down to the meadow, searching the trees and grass tufts and bushes, and soon discovered a bluebird's and a woodpecker's nest, and began an acquaintance with the frogs and snakes and turtles in the creeks and springs." John Muir (31)*

Daniel, Sarah, John, and David slept happily on the bare floor of their little, one room shanty that first night. Blankets and quilts, some borrowed from the Gray's, kept them warm enough through the cool, crisp night. Daniel woke before the light of dawn to build a fire in the new cast-iron stove. Soon, his commotions around the big stove and the smell of smoke flowing from around the fire door woke the rest of the family.

"Better git up and git going, children," Daniel said as he banged together some pans while unloading them from a large wooden moving box. "Welcome to our new home!" He scurried around looking for some food to cook.

Sarah quickly dressed and came to her father's rescue. "Let me do that, Papa." She found containers of dry beans and potatoes, placed some lard into the frying pan on the stove, and waited for the grease to heat for cooking.

"Boys, might as well get up and help!" John and David were already awake. The small, one room shanty left little room for anyone to have any privacy or quiet space.

"Yes, sir, Papa!" John quickly dressed in his very worn pants, wrinkled shirt, and all-around everyday work shoes. David also quickly dressed. Both boys were hungry and eager to eat whatever Sarah cooked and put before them. There were no chairs or stools to sit on, so the four stood around the small table next to the stove, filled their plates with beans and potatoes, and sat on the floor. Daniel said a long prayer of thanksgiving to bless the food and their new shanty house.

After breakfast, Daniel said to the children, "Mr. Gray and some neighbors are coming over today to help clear some land so we can cultivate it for planting. I hope to plant some corn and vegetables for us to live on. Later on, we'll begin to clear more of the land for planting wheat. While we're working, you three have lots of chores to do. Sarah, you, of course, need to unpack the food boxes, organize it so we can get to it, and plan a meal for supper. John and David, you two need to feed our little Indian bay, Jack, take him for a ride, and brush him down. Both of you need to help Sarah unpack the boxes of housewares and other things. Also, go down to the lake with your buckets and fetch some water for the water barrels."

"Yes, Papa!" John replied. David nodded in agreement. "Papa, when we finish our chores, can David and I wander around the woods and meadows? We're so excited to see every living, natural thing around our beautiful home!"

"Yes, you can, but only after you finish all the chores. Look around you, there's many, many things needing to be done. You don't have to look very far! Just use some common sense. First things first! You boys hear me?"

"Yes, Papa," John said.

"Yes, sir," David said with a big smile.

As soon as Daniel was out the door and out of sight, John and David ran to the tree holding the blue-jay's nest they'd seen the day before.

Natura flew directly over them to ensure John's safety. Natura scanned the surroundings, near and far, for any unusual energy vibrations that might mean an evil spirit was near.

Quickly reaching the tree, the boys climbed up to the nest. They found it empty! "How'd that happen so quickly, David?" John scratched his head through his over-grown red hair. "I can't imagine how the birds used their bills to move those little, thin, fragile eggs to another location!" (32)

"Well, John, somehow they did!" David looked a bit bewildered. "I mean, who else would do such a thing?"

"Don't know, David. Let's look for other nests before we do our chores."

They had no trouble finding many other nests, including blue-jays, brown thrushes, bluebirds, sparrows, kingbirds, hen-hawks, whip-poor-wills, and woodpeckers. Every time they found one, they'd whoop and holler like wild Indians on the warpath! They could spend the whole day doing this one thing!

Reluctantly, they soon returned to the shanty after finding several nests with eggs in them. They knew they had to do their chores, or suffer their father's wrath, which usually meant a painful whipping, along with very stern words of correction!

"We'd better go take care of pony Jack first," John said to David.

Jack was tied to a tree next to the shanty. Daniel had spread hay on the ground for him to lay on and to eat. Next to the hay pile was a bucket of water. As John and David walked closer to Jack, he became nervous, moved quickly away from the boys, and kicked the bucket, turning it upside down.

"Easy, Jack, take it easy. We're not going to hurt you." John stretched out his left hand to pat Jack's back while using his right hand to hold the rope.

"David, while I hold him, please untie the rope from the tree."

"Will do, John." David untied Jack's rope from the tree.

John slowly and gently led Jack away from the area, and moved toward a pathway leading to an open meadow on the east side of Fountain Lake. David followed close behind. Steadying and talking to Jack a final time, John, with his long legs, thrust himself upward and on-top of Jack, locking his legs around Jack's belly.

"Come on, David. Grab my hand and I'll pull you up so you can ride behind me."

David said not a word but grasped John's outstretched right hand, gave a big jump with both of his legs, and awkwardly straddled Jack just behind John.

"Good job, David. Now Jack, let's go toward the open meadow. Giddy up!"

Without hesitation, Jack obeyed John's command. He trotted very carefully and slowly along the path to the meadow's edge. Then, responding to John's foot kicks on both sides of his body and John's loosening of the rope, Jack began a steady gallop through the meadow and then circled around its perimeter. John and David held on for dear life!

After a few circles around the meadow, John headed Jack along the path to return to the shanty.

"Whoa, Jack!" John said. Jack stopped so suddenly that he threw the boys right over his head. Before they landed on the ground, Natura instantly blew a cushion of air under each boy to soften their landing. John and David shook off the dirt from their clothes, looked at each other, and roared with laughter! (33)

"Good boy, Jack!" John said. "Guess we gotta work on your stopping so quickly."

"Hold onto the rope, David, while I go fetch a bucket of water from the lake."

"Will do, John!" David replied, all excited from the fun ride on Jack, and even the sudden fall.

John soon returned with the bucket of water and placed it in front of Jack. Jack wasted no time drinking his fill of the fresh lake water. While he drank, John and David brushed Jack's sweat-soaked body with some brushes their father had told them to use.

"One chore done!" John said, talking to himself and also to David.

David just nodded as he made one last brush stroke down Jack's long tail.

"While we're getting more water for Jack, let's each take two buckets to the lake, fill them, and fill-up the large water barrel," John suggested. Both he and David grabbed two buckets each, walked down to Fountain Lake, filled them, and returned to the shanty to fill the water barrel. Several trips back and forth to the lake were necessary to completely fill the large barrel.

"Another chore done!" David announced happily.

"Let's go help Sarah unpack the large storage boxes," John said.

The two boys entered the small shanty to find Sarah on her knees, bent over a storage box filled with kitchen wares, pots, pans, and kettles. "What can we help you do, Sarah?" John asked, almost startling her.

"Oh, John and David! I'm glad it's you two and not one of the Indians! I tell you the truth, they really frighten me!"

"Oh, don't worry about them, Sarah," John replied. "Mr. Gray said they're harmless, although they are dirty and kind of wild. Just give a holler if you're ever frightened by one. David and I will come running to your rescue in no time at all."

"Why, thank you, John. That's comforting to know. Now, you asked what you can do. There're plenty of boxes of food packages you can unload and store on the shelves on either side of the stove. Try to organize the packages so we can tell what's what."

"Will do, Sarah," John replied.

"John, after you open the boxes, I'll hand the packages to you to place on the shelves. I'm not tall enough to reach the highest shelves," David said.

For the rest of the morning, Sarah, John, and David unpacked the large storage boxes of housewares and food packages, placing them on the shelves Daniel had hurriedly built the day before.

As John and David did their chores, they worked at a very slow pace and took plenty of time to look out at the most beautiful natural surroundings in the world! Sarah also enjoyed the outdoors but she was more interested in getting the storage boxes unpacked and organizing their contents so housewares, clothes, tools, dishes, and food could be easily found and used. She especially wanted to organize the kitchen area because she was fully responsible for the cooking. She had learned some cooking from her mother who'd given her several simple recipes to use. Mrs. Gray had also given her lessons in cooking on a wood-burning stove. But Sarah still felt like she was not fully trained and worried about her new role as the chief cook. She also saw herself as the 'woman of the house', at least on a temporary basis.

By mid-afternoon, John and David could no longer bare staying inside the crowded, little shanty. They just had to get outside and do some natural wandering of the vast wilderness surrounding their new home. Sarah was quite aware of the boys' feelings because they longingly looked out the shanty's only window and its front door, so much that they were useless helpers.

"John and David, if you want to take a long break and wander around outside, go ahead. I'm going to begin cooking supper and will need more room. The little space around the stove is too crowded for the three of us."

"Whish!" She thought she heard the wind blowing, turned around, and saw John and David running toward the dense woods surrounding the lake.

*"I guess I was right about how they felt,"* she thought to herself, and turned to select some food packages from the well-organized kitchen shelves. She had plenty of canned vegetables her mother and grandmother had prepared in Scotland. *"So, vegetable soup it'll be tonight. Now, if I can only remember how to make bread dough so I can bake some biscuits."*

As Sarah prepared supper, John and David wandered far into the woods to discover more bird nests. Panning his eyes across the tops of the trees, John saw a nest in the crook of a tall oak tree. He suddenly stopped! David, still looking up at the trees, bumped into John.

"Oops, John!"

"Let's be quiet, David! I can see a nest at the top of this oak tree. It's a pretty tall tree, but I think we can climb it. Let's see if we can find any eggs in the nest."

"Okay, John. You go first."

John peered up at the tall tree, found a limb to grab, and pulled himself up. Steadying himself on the first limb, he looked up and prepared to grab the next limb he could reach.

Feeling the disturbance John was making on the tree, one of the pair of hen-hawks peeked over the nest and spotted John and David at the bottom.

"Squawk! Squawk!" The hen-hawk yelled, as if it was calling out to someone. And it was. Flying overhead, soaring in wide circles, keeping a very close watch, was its mate. Seeing John halfway up the tree, clinging to a large limb, and David at the bottom getting ready to start his climb, the hovering hen-hawk quickly swooped down, first at John, and then at David, brushing its sharp talons across their heads, as if to say, "*Make one more move and I'll press my talons into your scalps!*" (34)

"Don't try to climb up, David! I'm coming down. We'd better find another tree to climb where there's a friendlier kind of bird!"

John scrambled down the tree. He and David looked up one more time at the angry hen-hawk, preparing to dive once again toward them. They ran as fast as they could toward a safer place!

Natura had hovered nearby John when he was up the tree. He had positioned his energy field next to him in order to buffer John from the angry hen-hawk. Had the hen-hawk come any closer to John, the energy field would have vibrated to a very high frequency. Upon sensing and feeling the high frequency, the hen-hawk would have been frightened away from John. Fortunately, John and David quickly scrambled down the tree. Natura breathed a sigh of relief even though he could have easily protected John from the hen-hawk. However, it would have been a little difficult to protect both John and David at the same time.

"That was a close call!" David said.

"It certainly was, David! Next time, we'd better do a better job of scanning the horizon to see if a bird, especially a hen-hawk, is flying nearby guarding the nest."

This close call by an angry hen-hawk didn't diminish their enthusiasm for searching for more bird nests. It just made their searching even more adventurous and exciting!

They soon spotted more bird nests belonging to birds that looked less threatening than the hen-hawk. But since the close call, they became more cautious, and watchful, before they climbed up any tree. Oftentimes, John and David just enjoyed being still and silent as they listened to the different songs of birds.

John and David thoroughly enjoyed those first few months of freedom, wandering endlessly it seemed, through the dense woods, far out into the meadows, and along the lake shore to discover birds, beavers, frogs, turtles, and even a few snakes who'd come to the water's edge to quench their thirst. However, those carefree days of wandering soon came to an end when Daniel decided that John and David were old enough to help make the farm.

A lot of work needed to be done that first summer to clear the land, cultivate it, and plant the seeds, in hopes of a good autumn harvest. Grandfather Gilrye's prophesy of hard, hard work was quickly coming to mind as Daniel began teaching the boys how to cut trees, clear heavy bushes and underbrush, pile the debris into high piles, and then set fire to it all. The huge fires burned for days it seems, and the cleared land slowly began to look like farm fields, ready for planting.

When Daniel had finished the planting, he started building a large frame house a short distance away from the one-room shanty. His wife, Anne, along with their other children, Margaret, Danny, Mary, and Anna were expected to arrive from Scotland in early November. The frame house had to be large enough for the whole family, so Daniel built a two and a half story house with eight rooms. He completed it in late October. Once he completed it, Sarah set about decorating it with white curtains along with wild flowers from the surrounding woods and meadows. Daniel also set about 'decorating' the yard by making a garden space for flowers in the front of the house. He and Sarah planted flowers using seeds he'd brought from Scotland. They also planted lilac bushes around the front porch.

# CHAPTER 13

## Daniel Meets Rest of Family in Milwaukee

*"Father was busy hauling lumber for the frame house that was to be got ready for the arrival of my mother, sisters, and brother, left behind in Scotland." John Muir (35)*

On the morning of October 30, 1849, Daniel, Sarah, John, and David woke earlier than usual, well before dawn, to prepare for Daniel's trip to Milwaukee to meet Anne and the four children. They were scheduled to arrive by way of a lake steamer in Milwaukee on November 4. When Daniel, Sarah, John, and David made their trip from Milwaukee to Kingston in April, it had taken them about a week to travel a distance of about a hundred miles. However, at that time, the weather was filled with heavy spring rains which made the pioneer roads especially muddy. In addition, their wagon was heavily loaded with them, their driver, and a large amount of household goods. Daniel hoped to make the trip to Milwaukee in five days because the roads would be drier and his wagon load would be lighter.

Daniel ate breakfast and packed a few large wooden boxes. Sarah helped him pack. In one box, they packed some food for Daniel to eat on his way to Milwaukee and for the whole family to eat when they returned to Fountain Lake. In another box, they packed pillows, quilts, and blankets. Daniel would use these for sleeping when he stopped each night to camp. The bedding would also be used for Anne and the children for keeping warm on their long journey home.

John and David readied two pairs of large horses with harnesses, reins, collars, and mouth bits, and then hitched them to a large wagon. Daniel had borrowed the horses from Alexander Gray because he only had two plough horses, Nob and Nell, and of course, the pony, Jack.

Daniel slowly guided the four horses along a very familiar road toward Kingston. Although the road was well-traveled by many farmers going to and from Kingston for supplies, it was fairly rough and filled with plenty of ruts and potholes. The Wisconsin county governments were very new and public road building and maintenance plans were still being developed. However, Daniel hoped that the main roads beyond Kingston, going south to Milwaukee, would be better. But he soon learned that they were not. He did the best he could guiding the horses and wagon around the largest ruts and holes. He didn't push the horses very hard because they had a long, long trip to make and therefore needed to take it easy. He stopped every hour or so to rest the horses, water them, and to also rest himself.

After four long days of travel, he thought he was getting close to Milwaukee because the traffic of travelers seemed to be increasing. He began looking for a good place to stop and camp for the last night. Soon he reached the little village of Menomonee Falls on the outskirts of Milwaukee. Daniel became excited as he soon found a suitable campsite on the Menomonee River. It was a good place for watering the horses and for sleeping near the calming sounds of the small river stream.

Meanwhile, back home in Marquette County, Sarah, John, and David were very excited anticipating the arrival of their mother and four siblings. Sarah was continuing to put the final decorative touches on their new house in preparation for their arrival. She was also very busy baking bread loaves, scones, and pies to have ready for eating. There wasn't much John and David could do to help Sarah with the baking, so they took the opportunity of this freedom to explore the dense woods, large open meadows, and everything natural around Fountain Lake.

Anne and the four children, Margaret, Danny, Mary, and Anna woke early on the morning of November 4 as their lake steamer sailed across Lake Michigan to Milwaukee. Daniel also woke very early. He hitched up the horses to the wagon at Menomonee Falls before sun-up and slowly headed for the Milwaukee lakefront to meet Anne and the children at the passenger pier.

After several hours of steady traveling, Daniel reached the city limits of Milwaukee. Stopping at the first livery stable he saw to water and rest the horses, Daniel asked the owner for directions to the lakefront and ship passenger pier. Now with good directions in hand, he confidently traveled directly through the bustling downtown area and soon arrived at the waterfront area. Since he, Sarah, John, and David had arrived at this same area only nine months ago, Daniel was very familiar with it. He soon found a parking space for his horses and wagon a few blocks the main passenger pier.

Several lake steamers were docked at the pier and passengers were busy either loading or unloading from a few of them. Daniel carefully observed the passengers unloading for any signs of Anne, Margaret, Danny, Mary, and Anna. Not seeing them, he walked to the passenger ticket office to inquire when the next lake steamer would arrive from Buffalo. Before he could ask the ticket agent, he noticed out of a corner of his left eye that a steamer was fast approaching the lakefront from the northeast of Lake Michigan.

"Yes sir, what can I do for you, Mister?"

"I'm expecting my family to arrive today aboard a steamer from Buffalo. Can you tell me when it is scheduled to arrive?"

"Well, sir, that'll be the steamer you now see approaching from the northeast. She should arrive at the passenger pier in about ten minutes."

"Thank you, sir!"

Excitement and emotions quickly filled Daniel as he walked closer to the passenger exit gate at the pier. He found it hard to stand still and wait. He paced back and forth while keeping his eyes on the lake steamer as the captain carefully maneuvered her through the harbor channel toward an empty pier near the main passenger terminal. Daniel now could see deck hands gathering at the rails with large ropes in their hands, ready to toss them to the pier hands waiting to securely tie the ropes to the large pier-anchor posts.

Now securely docked, the pier hands moved a large stairs platform to the middle of the steamer so passengers could disembark. Many passengers were now gathered along the rails. Several passengers waived and shouted at their family members standing outside the terminal gates! The family members, of course, waived and shouted with great excitement in return!

One by one, the passengers began stepping down the exit stairway. Daniel looked carefully at each one, particularly looking for Anne and the four children.

*"There they are!"* Daniel said aloud to himself.

Waving both arms and shouting as loud as he could, Anne now caught sight of Daniel. She too began to wave with one hand while holding onto the stairway railing with the other. She turned to the four children to tell them about their father's location. Now seeing their father, each of the children waved with both of their hands.

Finally, the passengers quickly moved through the exit gate where they were welcomed by their family members.

Daniel and Anne ran toward each other; the children followed close behind Anne.

Now embracing each other, Daniel said to Anne, "Oh dear Anne, how wonderful to see you! It has been much too long since we've been together!"

"It surely has been a long time, Daniel!" She and Daniel hugged and kissed each other.

The children quickly encircled Daniel and hugged his legs as tightly as they could.

"Oh, dear children! What a sight for sore eyes! My, how you've grown!" Daniel picked each of the four children up, one at a time, and gave them hugs and kisses.

Similar greetings and excited gatherings could be seen throughout the passenger terminal.

After the welcome and much chatter about the long ocean voyage, the Muir family walked to the luggage area where pier hands were unloading baggage from one of the steamer's side doors.

Daniel returned to the horses and wagon and moved them to a platform near the passenger terminal where all the baggage was placed. A few pier hands helped Daniel load the family's baggage onto his large wagon. After the baggage was loaded, Anne and the four children climbed aboard the wagon.

"I just can't believe we're all together again! Praise be to the Lord!" Daniel said to this family.

"How true and right, Daniel!" Anne replied. "No words can express our joy!"

"Now, my dear family, we still have a long journey ahead of us," Daniel said. "Try to be patient and as comfortable as you can be on this old wagon. We have plenty of food and warm blankets to keep us comfortable for the trip. We'll stop periodically to rest and water the horses, along with resting ourselves. We'll also camp out each night. I've found some very good camping sites near some small villages that should be ideal for us."

And away they went on their not too long of a journey to their new home on beautiful Fountain Lake.

# CHAPTER 14

## Visits by an Indian and an Evil Spirit

*"Indians belonging to the Menominee and Winnebago tribes occasionally visited us at our cabin to get a piece of bread or some matches, or to sharpen their knives on our grindstone, and we boys watched them closely to see that they didn't steal Jack. We wondered at their knowledge of animals when we saw them go direct to trees on our farm, chop holes in them with their tomahawks and take out a coon, of the existence of which we had never noticed the slightest trace. In winter, after the first snow, we frequently saw three or four Indians hunting deer in company, running like hounds on the fresh exciting tracks. The escape of the deer from these noiseless, tireless hunters was said to be well-nigh impossible; they were followed to the death." John Muir (36)*

Back at Fountain Lake, all was going very well as Sarah, John, and David prepared for the arrival of their family from Milwaukee. It was now November 8, a day before Daniel thought he, Anne, and the four children would arrive home.

John jumped out of bed before dawn, too excited to sleep knowing that the entire Muir family would be together in a few days.

"Get up, David! Let's get the cooking stove fired up for Sarah, grab some breakfast, and feed the animals. If Sarah doesn't need our help, we'll have the whole day to find new bird nests!"

"Sounds good to me, John!" David quickly pulled on his pants and jumped into his shoes.

John and David soon ran out the door toward the shanty, now converted into a small barn. Along with the farm tools, other farm supplies and feed for the farm animals, the kindling for the cooking stove was also stored in the little shanty-barn. Returning to the house with the wood, they soon had a roaring fire going in the stove's firebox which provided heat to the stove-top.

"Thanks, John and David!" Sarah placed pans and skillets on the four burners on top of the stove. "I'll finish preparing today's lunch and dinner for us. The bread, scones, and pies are already baked for the homecoming of our family tomorrow. I'll just need to cook the wild turkey Papa killed, along with potatoes, squash, and green beans."

"No problem, Sarah!" David replied. "We'll be close at hand. Just ring the dinner bell twice if you need us. We always hear it loud and clear!"

"Yes, Sarah," John said. "We won't venture very far away, and will come around often to make sure you're safe."

"Thanks, John and David. I just don't trust the local Indians just yet."

John and David ran out the door and headed toward the north end of Fountain Lake to watch the beavers build a dam.

In only a few minutes, they were huffing and puffing, as they peered through the bushes to see two beavers busily working on their dam. Both beavers would swim to the nearest bank, find a fallen tree limb, grab it by their large front teeth, and swim back to the dam to place it carefully in just the right place to build the dam. Time after time, for about an hour, the two beavers continued to bring tree limbs to add to their dam. If they couldn't find loose limbs, they'd cut down a small tree with their sharp teeth to create a supply. John and David were mesmerized. They quietly watched and enjoyed the two animals as they built their winter home.

"Dong! Dong!" They heard the dinner bell ring!

"Sarah needs us, David! Let's hurry home!"

Quickly they ran along the trail on the west side of the lake. Both boys were fast runners. They'd promised Sarah they would stay close to home in case she needed them. Looks like she needed them now!

Within only a few minutes, they were at the steps of their new house. Sarah was standing on the front porch next to the dinner bell. Next to her was one of the local Indians holding a basket with one hand and a spear in the other. He had a tomahawk hanging from a leather belt around his waist.

"What's up, Sarah?" John asked as he and David stepped onto the porch and stood next to Sarah. She looked very relieved to see them.

"Well, John, this Indian is asking for some food and other things. I really can't understand what he's saying. He knows I'm alone because he saw Papa leave a week ago, and then he probably saw you two leave this morning."

At this, the Indian backed away down the steps, still holding the basket and spear.

"Here's what we'll do, Sarah," John said. "David and I will stay here on the porch while you go into the house and get a few food items to place in the Indian's basket. Afterward, we'll all wave our hands at him as if to say 'goodbye'. Hopefully, he'll turn and leave. If not, I'll grab father's shotgun from the down stairs closet and aim it over his head."

"Sounds like a good plan, John," Sara slowly turned, went into the house, grabbed a few loaves of bread and some canned goods, returned to the porch, and placed them into the Indian's basket.

With that, John, David, and Sarah waved their hands into the air as if to say goodbye.

The Indian got the message. He looked into his basket and bowed his head as if to say thank-you, turned around, and walked slowly into the woods.

"Whew!" Sarah breathed a sigh of relief. "That was a close one! I didn't know what to do. I think he knew I was alone. He seemed determined to have his basket filled, one way or another!"

"Maybe so, Sarah," John replied. "We just don't know what his intentions were. I'm just glad you rang the bell for David and I to come home!"

"Me too, John. Thanks to you and David for staying close by and coming to my rescue. Please promise me you'll stay near the house the rest of the day."

"We will," David replied.

Unknown to John, David, and Sarah, Natura was hovering overhead during the entire episode. He was ready to defend the whole family, if necessary. He didn't have a plan but he knew he'd be assisted by many others angels if he needed them.

As they watched the Indian disappear into the woods, Natura saw a streak of brilliant light flash where the Indian had entered the woods. He wondered if an evil spirit had prompted the Indian to do what he did. "*Could the Indian be possessed by an evil spirit?*"

John and David continued their wanderings but stayed close by the house to keep Sarah company and safe. Natura stayed very close to John, and of course, David.

To be sure the Indian with the basket didn't return to their house, John and David followed his trail into the woods in the direction of what is called the West Bank, staying close enough to see or hear him, but hopefully out of his sight. The Indian walked slowly along a trail that goes over the bank, then deeper into the woods west of the Muir house. When John and David climbed up the bank, they had a commanding view of the north end of Fountain Lake. They clearly saw the Indian cross a small spring stream coming into the lake. He suddenly stopped, took his long spear, and thrust it into a muskrat's home located next to the shoreline. They saw the Indian hold the spear with one hand while he used his tomahawk to dig down into the home to find the muskrat on the end of the spear, and then kill it with his tomahawk. After throwing the dead muskrat over his shoulder, the Indian continued walking northeast in the meadow near the Fox River. Feeling assured that the Indian was truly going away from their house, the boys turned around to go home.

Suddenly, John tripped on what appeared to be a large root connected to an old oak tree. Natura immediately saw that the 'large root' was really an evil spirit stretching itself out intentionally to trip John. He must have left the Indian and stayed on the trail hoping to find a way to harm John.

*"Why would any evil spirit want to do that?"* Natura quickly thought.

Natura rushed to John's aid by positioning his body underneath John to cushion his fall. John also helped himself by extending his hands out to the ground to help brace his body.

"You, evil spirit, cease your evil ways and leave this place!" Natura shouted, using his spiritually-energized voice.

Serpenta partly emerged and moved quickly from the ground beneath John and hovered above him. He hoped to find another opportunity to hurt John in the pretense that John's own tripping caused his own injury.

Now partly visible, appearing as a black cloud over John's body, Serpenta laughed crazily and responded to Natura, "You win this round, Natura, because you have spiritual power greater than mine. But mark my word, when you're absent from John's presence for only a second, I'll have my way with him before you can stop me!" With that, the black cloud with Serpenta simply disappeared. John brushed himself off and stood up, wondering what had just happened.

"John, are you alright?" David asked. "You seemed to have fallen over that tree root but I couldn't actually see how you did it. All I could see is you seeming to trip and then falling to the ground."

"Not sure what happened, David, but I'm okay, just a little dumbfounded by it all."

John and David continued walking on the trail toward their house. They didn't want Sarah to be alone for very long.

# CHAPTER 15

## The Muir Family Reunites

*"The ninth of this month is the anniversary of my arrival at Fountain Lake twenty years ago. How happy I was to meet you (John) and the others after such a long journey." Anne Muir (37)*

*"We moved into our frame house in the autumn, when mother with the rest of the family arrived from Scotland, and, when the winter snow began to fly, our bur-oak shanty was made into a stable for Jack." John Muir (38)*

It was now November 9, 1849, the day their father was expected to return from Milwaukee with the rest of the family. Sarah, John, and David woke earlier than usual, hardly able to sleep thinking about the family's arrival. As usual, John and David fetched some kindling wood from the shanty-barn and started a fire in the kitchen stove.

Afterward, John asked Sarah, "Is there anything else David and I can help you do today?"

"No thanks, John. I've got everything ready to cook. You and David can go wandering, or whatever you want to do. I do want you to stay close to the house in case I need you for something. I don't want to feel alone or without any help if I need you."

"Okay, Sarah. We won't venture too far. First, we have to feed and water the animals. We'll also have to brush the horses and oxen down, and take them outside for some exercise activity. After that, we'll need to cut-up plenty of wood for the fireplace and cooking stove. The temperature isn't so cold just yet, but I'm sure winter's freezing weather is lurking nearby ready to put a chill on us."

"Thanks, John and David, for all your help. I can't wait to have our family all together tonight when they return from Milwaukee!"

"Me too!" David replied.

"Yes, we'll have a great time tonight celebrating our wonderful reunion!" John said.

John and David went to the shanty-barn, now very crowded with pony Jack; two work-horses, Nob and Nell; two oxen, Tom and Jerry, and two milk-cows, who they hadn't yet named.

"David, let's fetch some water for all seven of them. Afterward, we can spread some fresh hay around for them to eat, and also fill their feeders with fresh oats. We'll also have to milk the two cows and feed the chickens."

"Sounds like a great plan to me, John."

When the boys had completed the feeding, they each grabbed a brush used for cleaning the manes and hides of the large stock animals.

"David, you can brush pony Jack and I'll brush Nob and Nell. Then, we can both brush Tom and Jerry."

"Okay, John."

John and David both worked very hard to brush the dirt and burrs from the large animals. As they brushed, they spoke soothingly to each animal as if they were family pets, which they were to some degree. But Daniel forbade them from petting the livestock, except for pony Jack, because he looked upon them as 'animals of burden' created by God to do hard farm work. He didn't want the children becoming too affectionate with them.

After the brushing of the animals, the boys bridled and harnessed them, preparing them to do some work.

"David, let's hitch Nob and Nell to the wagon and use them to haul pumpkins from the fields to our new home. Papa said we should store as many as we can in the basement so we can eat them over the winter months."

John and David worked for a few hours loading the pumpkins on a little wagon and hauling them to the house for storage in the basement. Later, they hitched Tom and Jerry, yoked them together, and led them to the nearby woods to pull some downed trees to the shanty-barn.

John was already an excellent tree cutter and wood splitter. With John doing all of the trimming and splitting, and David stacking the wood, the boys soon had a large pile of kindling and split-logs neatly stacked up against the shanty-barn.

"After all of our hard work, it's time to have some fun, David!" John returned the axes and splitting-wedge to their rightful place in the shanty-barn.

"Do you mean what I think you mean, John? Like taking pony Jack out for a good ride?"

"You would be correct, David!"

By now, John and David knew how to ride Jack bareback without any bridle or rope. They just used their legs and feet as pressure on Jack's sides to guide him either to the right or to the left. They also learned to lean a little one way or the other to guide him. Jack had also gotten used to their riding and followed their gentle guidance like they were all bound together as one flesh and spirit.

"Way to go, Jack!" John encouraged their brave Indian pony as he and David wildly rode at full speed over the open meadow made by melting glaciers thousands of years ago.

David, riding behind John, hung onto him with both arms. "Whoopee! Gitty up, brave pony Jack!"

After four or five times of galloping around the huge meadow area, they slowed Jack down and guided him toward the shanty-barn. Dismounting one by one, they were happy they'd learned to stop Jack without flying over his head and landing hard on the ground. John called it 'that flying method of dismounting'!

John and David gave Jack plenty of water and also brushed him down once again.

"Good Jack! Good Jack!" John said, as he and David lovingly brushed Jack's mane and body as he cooled down from the long, hard ride.

Caring for the livestock and cutting the firewood had taken John and David several hours to complete. But they still had one chore to do before calling it a day.

"Well, David, let's fill the water barrels with fresh lake water. We'll soon have seven Muirs under one roof who'll need both drinking and bathing water."

John and David each carried two empty buckets rigged to a yoked-like wooden piece around their neck and shoulders. After several trips to and from the lake, they soon had filled the two large water barrels next to the house's front porch.

Now stepping onto the porch, John announced, "We're home, Sarah. We'll be at the shanty-barn, feeding Jack and brushing him down."

"Okay, thanks John, I know. I saw you and David filling the water barrels."

It was now about 5:30 p.m.; the sun was beginning to set. Sarah had finished cooking the dinner meal and was now keeping it warm on the stove top. John and David were now sitting on the front porch. Sara decided to join them to wait and watch for their family to arrive.

Each of them began to look up the long driveway leading to Gillette Road for any signs of their father's four horses and large wagon, which would carry their father, mother, and four siblings. They listened for any sounds of the horses and wagon. However, they didn't know that it would be a few hours yet before their family's arrival. They lit some candles in the kitchen and living room. The candles' lights shined through the open front door to light the front porch where they continued to wait and watch for the rest of the family to arrive. Their excitement grew as each minute passed, wondering what it'd be like with all of the Muir family together after nine months of separation.

Around eight o'clock, they began to hear the sounds of the wagon wheels as they rolled along Gillette Road. Then they could hear talking and laughing from Daniel, Anne, and their four siblings. They could see the light from the wagon's lantern grow brighter through the dense woods as the wagon came closer. When

Daniel pulled the reins of the horses toward the driveway, he and the family saw the candle lights from the house and felt great joy and relief to finally be at their new American home!

Sarah, John, and David got up from the porch and ran toward the wagon to greet their entire family. Hardly waiting for Daniel to stop the wagon, the children jumped from the wagon to greet Sarah, John, and David. Anne stayed on the wagon with Daniel until he safely stopped the horses next to the porch. Anne carefully climbed down from the wagon, quickly walked toward the children, and hugged Sarah, John, and David ever so tightly!

"Oh Sarah, John, and David, how wonderful to see you, and especially to hug you!" Anne gave each child a strong hug. She then kissed each on their cheeks.

Anne briefly stepped back. "My, how each of you have grown!

Suddenly, Margaret, Danny, Mary, and Anna gathered around Sarah, John, and David, jumping and squealing like 'wild Indians'. Each one took turns hugging one another and chattering non-stop about their adventures. Sarah, John, and David told about how they helped father make their new home. The other children shared their tales of their long journey across the Atlantic, the rivers and canals, and the Great Lakes.

After enjoying their greeting, Sarah announced that supper was waiting for them in the kitchen. The entire Muir family entered the new house for the first time. They seated themselves at the large kitchen table. Daniel said a long prayer of thanksgiving before they all filled their plates to eat. The family talked non-stop about their adventures coming to America and to their new home. Afterward, Daniel gathered them into the living room where he held a prayer meeting to thank God for their new home and for the reunion of their entire family. He also talked with them about the chores each of them would be assigned to do beginning the next day.

# CHAPTER 16

## The Making of the Muir Farm

*"I was first put to burning brush in clearing land for the plough. Those magnificent brush fires with great white hearts and red flames, the first big, wild outdoor fires I had ever seen, were wonderful sights for young eyes. Again, and again, when they were burning fiercest so that we could hardly approach near enough to throw another branch, father put them to awfully practical use as warning lessons, comparing their heat with that of hell, and the branches with bad boys...I was put to the plough at the age of twelve, when my head reached but little above the handles, and for many years I had to do the greater part of the ploughing. It was hard work for so small a boy; nevertheless, as good ploughing was from me as if I were a man, and very soon I had become a good ploughman, or rather ploughboy...And as I was the eldest boy, the greater part of all the other hard work of the farm quite naturally fell on me. I had to split rails for long lines of zigzag fences." John Muir (39)*

The next morning, the family woke early and gathered in the kitchen for their first breakfast at their new home. Anne and Sarah worked in the kitchen to prepare breakfast. Sarah was proud to show her mother how to use the new cooking stove and, of course, to show her how well she could now cook.

"Let us bow our heads to thank God," Daniel said to his family, now all together for the first time in nine months.

"Dear Heavenly Father, we give thanks for this family, for each and every one, for taking care of us during our long separation, for giving us all safe travel from Scotland to America, and for this first breakfast together at our new home. We praise you for guiding and protecting us and we ask you to continue to do so. We thank you for this bountiful food we're about to eat and for the hands that prepared it, my dear wife, Anne, and my dear daughter, Sarah. We especially thank you for Sarah's, John's and David's wonderful work in helping to make this a beautiful home in which to live and grow. In the name of Jesus, we pray. Amen."

Plates of biscuits, pancakes, bacon, potatoes, and scrambled eggs were passed around the large table. Fresh milk in a large pitcher was also passed around the table. Anne had prepared a fresh pot of coffee for Daniel and herself, and also for the oldest children who might like to drink it. As the large Muir family ate, they talked non-stop about their experiences over the last nine months. Daniel, Sarah, John, and David were excited to tell about their long trip across the Atlantic, and Anne and the four other children told about their long voyage also. Everyone was so happy to be in America and especially in their new farm home on Fountain Lake.

After breakfast, Daniel proudly took the family on a tour of the farm, beautiful Fountain Lake, and the large meadow where he'd planted a field of winter wheat. John and David gave them a tour of the trail around Fountain Lake.

"Look everybody," David said, pointing to the piles of limbs and brush in the lake, "those are the homes of the beavers and muskrats. John and I watched as some of them were being built!"

As the family passed through the forest, John pointed to several trees saying, "Over there at that large oak tree is where David and I found our first blue jays nest. And over there at the top of the sugar maple is where we found our first blue bird's nest!"

When they returned from their tour of the farm, Daniel gathered the family together for another prayer meeting to give thanks to God for their new home. "Now Anne and children, gather round as I tell you what work has to be done to prepare the house, the farm, the animals, and ourselves for the coming winter. Everybody has to do something, even the youngest children." Daniel looked adoringly at Mary and Anna, the little twin girls (age 3), and little Danny (age 6).

He also discussed with the family the work that each of them was expected to do. Anne and the girls would work in the house to organize all of the clothing, bedding, and other personal things so everybody could easily find them. Anne, Margaret, and Sarah would store the large food pantry with canned food, flour, and salted meat. They'd also help harvest the potatoes and store them in the cellar.

"John and David, since you're the oldest boys, you'll be expected to do all of the outside chores. We'll need to harvest the corn and potatoes right away, and later on harvest the winter wheat. You'll also need to cut and store enough firewood in the barn so your mother can cook for us all winter."

Not forgetting about little Danny, the youngest boy at age six, Daniel said, "There's plenty of work for you to do in helping John, David, and me with our work. We'll need you to fetch tools for us and also to help feed pony Jack, the horses, the oxen, the cows, and the chickens."

Looking very happy to have his own work to do, little Danny smiled proudly.

When winter came with its cold temperatures and deep snow, Daniel woke the family at six o'clock. Before the boys ate breakfast, they had to feed the horses, oxen, cows, and chickens; sharpen the axes and other tools; bring in firewood for cooking; and other chores. After breakfast, they had to go out into the cold, snowy weather to cut trees, trim the trees into fencing length logs, and then build zigzag fences.

In early December, before the cold weather and snow began, a heavy rain started in the middle of the night, waking the boys from their sound sleep. All three boys slept together in a regular size bed in an upstairs bedroom.

"Listen, David and Danny!" John said. "Do you hear what I hear? Sounds like a good heavy rain, which means we might have the day to ourselves. We certainly can't get outside to do any work!"

"You're right, John!" David replied. "I can't wait to have some time inside to build things with my wooden blocks!"

"Me too!" Little Danny chimed in. "Can I help you build something, David?"

"You sure can!"

"Well, I think I'll do some reading," John said. "I've borrowed some great novels from our neighbor, Bradley Brown. I can't wait to begin reading them!"

Little did the boys know that their father had other work for them to do on this rainy day. When the family sat down for breakfast, Daniel prayed his usual very long blessing, almost a sermon in itself, and the family began eating. Even in the heavy rains or snowstorms, Daniel always had work for them to do.

"Well, my fine laddies, today's heavy rain means that we'll have to find work inside."

John, David, and little Danny looked at each other with disappointing faces.

"Since we can't work outside, we'll all work in the barn. We've got plenty of corn to shuck and shell, axe-handles and ox-yokes to make, and there's plenty of mending to do. Now girls, this is also a good time for you to help with the farm chores. When you've finished helping your mother, come out to the barn and help with the fanning and thrashing of the winter wheat. You can also help sort the potatoes, brush the dirt from them, and take them down to the cellar for winter storage."

Daniel gave his family very little time to rest or just take it easy. He was always possessed with work, work, work, and then worship, worship, worship. The family had precious little time to just rest or relax. The whole family had to sacrifice much to build the farm and make a living. In some ways, their bodies suffered much because they worked so hard. John's growth was affected so much that he didn't grow as normal boys should, David became faint and dizzy doing many chores, while both Sarah and Margaret suffered so much in their bodies that their adult health declined at early ages, causing them to lose some normal abilities for living a happy, healthy life. It was not until Daniel became an old man that he realized his past mistakes and regretted working his children so hard. He was especially bothered by his overbearing treatment of John.

Natura stayed busy during each work day, looking after John, and the rest of the family as they worked close to John. He watched John very closely, knowing that John was working too hard for any boy, or any man around Marquette County. Natura couldn't necessarily help reduce the workload but he could keep John from injuring himself.

When spring came, John began ploughing the fields for planting. He could hardly see above the plough handles but he persevered. Natura helped and supported him as he ploughed. For many years, John did much of the ploughing. He could plough a furrow as straight as anyone around the county. John also became one of the county's best tree choppers and stump-diggers. (40)

One day, as John was leaning over on his knees, chopping through oak and hickory stumps, his father walked up to check on him. "Now, John, I know that's hard, hard work, but it'll do you good. For God made us to do hard work. Some day when you grow up to be a man, you'll look back and appreciate what you've done!"

"Yes, Papa." John wiped the sweat from his brow. "I guess you're right, but at the rate I'm going, I'm not sure I'll be around 'til manhood." John was now digging deep down below the crowns of the big roots, some two feet or more in diameter.

"Don't you worry, John, you'll survive, because our good Lord will provide."

John didn't know it at the time but he was developing the physical skills that would be useful to him when he made his wilderness explorations later in life. Daniel allowed no time for his children to recreate, have fun, and just do things as normal children do. He saw no need for any other activities beyond farm work, Bible study, and worship. He was also very strict about making the children go to bed early, and of course, rise early the next day.

# CHAPTER 17

## Swimming, Boating, and Fishing on Fountain Lake

*"Our beautiful lake, named Fountain Lake by father, but Muir's Lake by the neighbours, is one of the many small glacier lakes that adorn the Wisconsin landscapes. It is fed by twenty or thirty meadow springs, is about half a mile long, half as wide and surrounded by low finely-modelled hills dotted with oak and hickory, and meadows full of grasses and sedges and many beautiful orchids and ferns...We always had to work hard, but if we worked still harder we were occasionally allowed a little spell in the long summer evenings about sundown to fish, and on Sundays an hour or two to sail quietly without fishing-rod or gun when the lake was calm. Therefore, we gradually learned something about its inhabitants--pickerel, sunfish, black bass, perch, shiners, pumpkin-seeds, ducks, loons, turtles, muskrat, etc...On Sundays, after or before chores and sermons and Bible-lessons, we drifted about the lake for hours, especially in lily time, getting finest lessons and sermons from the water and flowers, ducks, fishes and muskrats...One hot summer day father told us that we ought to learn to swim. This was one of the most interesting suggestions he had ever offered, but precious little time was allowed for trips to the lake, and he seldom tried to show us how." John Muir (41)*

Infrequently it seems, Daniel's heart would feel a tug of compassion for his hard-working boys. On a hot summer day one year, after the boys had worked hard in the fields, he decided they should cool themselves in lake. "Boys, go down to the lake and jump in to cool yourselves! While you're at it, I think it's time you learned to swim."

"Oh, thank you Papa!" John quickly replied. "That sounds like a great idea! Will you show how to swim?"

"You know I don't have the time for such! All you have to do is watch the frogs. They'll teach you all you need to know about swimming. You'll see how easily they push themselves along by paddling their arms and kicking their strong little legs. Just imitate them and you'll be swimming before you know it." (42)

"Oh, that sounds like fun, Papa!" David said, as he stretched his arms in front of him and made swimming-like strokes.

"Danny, you can go with John and David to splash around in the shallow area while they practice their swimming, but be careful you don't go into the deep part just yet. Once John and David learn to be good swimmers, they can teach you. John and David, keep your eyes on Danny and don't let him venture too far out into the lake!"

"Yes, Papa," John replied. "David and I will watch after him, and also watch after each other. Won't we David?"

"Sure will, John!" David continued make swimming-like strokes in the hot, summer air.

The boys ran down to a little basin on the south end of the lake, removed their hot, sweaty work clothes except for their underwear, and waded into the chilly water among the rushes. John and David quickly ventured out to about waist deep water while Danny was content to splash around in water next to the shore. It was in this little basin that John and David practiced one of their many swimming lessons, keeping in mind how they saw the frogs swimming. Day after day during their first summer, they continued their lessons and soon were able to swim around the basin without touching the bottom.

That same summer, Daniel gave the boys enough pine boards to make a small row boat. John's talents for designing machines and clocks began to surface around this time. (43) With pencil and paper in hand one night, he sketched out a boat design suitable enough to use in building a little boat. Cutting the boards into precise pieces and tacking them together with nails, John and David then wedged rope into the spaces where the pieces came together, melted tar in an old iron pot on the kitchen stove, and then carefully poured the tar along the rope lines until they had a 'waterproof' boat. For the most part, the launch of the little boat was successful but some water seeped in here and there. Each time it did, the boys would return to shore, melt more tar, and pack it carefully around the leaky spots until no more water seeped into the boat.

On Sundays, when the boys had some free time, they'd row out into the middle of the lake, place the oars inside the boat, and drift around the lake for hours to wherever the wind took them. John declared that he and his brothers were "*getting (the) finest lessons and sermons from the water and flowers, ducks, fishes and muskrats*" as they got from their father's Bible-lessons. (44)

On July fourth of that summer, John received the scare of his life when he almost drowned trying to swim in the deeper water. One of the Larson boys was visiting and they decided to go fishing in their little boat. After reaching deep water well beyond their little swimming basin, John and David jumped into the water for a swim while the Larson boy stay onboard to fish. David stayed near the boat while John ventured out to where the water was twenty or thirty feet deep.

*"Now I can really swim like a fish in this deep water!"* John thought to himself as he glided effortless across the crystal, clear water.

After swimming for away from the boat for twenty yards or so, he decided it was time to return to the safety of the boat. As usual, Natura was hovering or swimming right along with John, just in case John needed help.

*"It's time for me to see how far I can swim underwater,"* John thought.

He took a very deep breath of fresh air and dove deeply under the water, swimming directly toward the boat where the Larson boy and David now sat. They were facing the opposite direction, only a little aware of where John was had swam, and not aware that he was now returning to the boat, underwater.

"*Just a little more, John. You can make it,*" he thought. Natura also thought, "*I hope he can!*"

As John swam toward the stern of the boat, he reached up with his right arm to grab the boat. But he missed! Serpenta made sure that he did by pushing the boat away from John. As he missed, the downward thrust of his arms and his momentum pulled him deeper and deeper into the water, until he feet reached the lake's bottom.

"*What's happening to me!*" John thought as he struggled, frightened and confused, to regain control of his body.

Natura immediately saw what Serpenta had done by pushing the boat away from John. He then saw John struggling, then sinking to the bottom of the lake. He swiftly moved his body under John to lift him toward the surface. However, before Natura could get John to the surface, John suddenly kicked wildly away, still frightened, thinking he was surely drowning! And he was! Once again, Natura raced through the deep water to place his body, now with his wings outstretched, under John. With his mighty strength, Natura quickly raised John to the surface once again and held onto him very tightly so he didn't slip away as before.

"*My mind is finally clearing!*" John thought. "*I can now reach the boat!*"

With both hands on the boat, and with Natura pushing and lifting him, John gasped for his breath and asked for help. The Larson boy and David quickly grabbed hold of John's arms and pulled him into the boat. Natura, of course, was continuing to push and lift John as well.

Looking very frightened with a wild-eyed look on his face, John breathed deeply in and out, while coughing up some lake water that went into his lungs.

"What happened, John!" David shouted, knowing that John didn't look well and was certainly struggling to get into the boat.

"I just gave out of air and breathed in some water! That's all!"

John was very humiliated and asked the boys to keep it a secret. But Sarah had heard John's call for help while she was working in the flower garden in front of the house.

When the boys arrived at the lake shore and walked up to the house, Sarah asked, "John, I heard you calling for help that you couldn't get out of the water. Were you drowning!"

The Larson boy and David looked at each other. Then the Larson boy quickly came up with a reply to protect John by saying, "No, he wasn't drowning, Sarah. He was just having some fun with David and me!" (45)

Natura hovered around the children and listened to the conversation, knowing that John would have surely drowned if he had not helped John. He also knew that John would have probably made it to the boat if Serpenta hadn't pushed it away.

John was definitely moved by this near-drowning experience. He was very ashamed of himself. At night before going to sleep, he carefully reviewed the event in detail and concluded that there was no good reason for him to lose control of himself in water. He vowed he'd never let it happen again! Time after time, he'd row the little boat out to the middle of the lake, anchor it, remove his clothes, and dive into the deep water. Straight down, he'd dive thirty or forty feet, turn easily around while dragging his feet on the bottom, and paddle to the surface.

"There, take that, water!" John would shout, hitting the water with his hands, and then swim around the boat in a victory lap of sorts. Accomplishing this victory was ever so sweet for John and taught him to persevere in overcoming his fears and prepared him for his future adventures as a mountaineer. (46)

# CHAPTER 18

## A New Farm, A Dangerously-Deep Well

*"A well ninety feet deep had to be dug, all except the first ten feet or so in fine-grained sandstone. When the sandstone was struck, my father, on the advice of a man who had worked mines, tried to blast the rock; but from lack of skill the blasting went on very slowly, and father decided to have me do all the work with mason's chisels, a long, hard job, with a good deal of danger in it. I had to sit cramped in a space about three feet in diameter, and wearily chip, chip, with heavy hammer and chisels from early morning until dark, day after day, for weeks and months. In the morning, father and David lowered me in a wooden bucket by a windlass, hauled up what chips were left from the night before, then went away to the farm work and left me until noon, when they hoisted me out for dinner. After dinner I was promptly lowered again, the forenoon's accumulation of chips hoisted out of the way, and I was left until night." John Muir. (47)*

As the children became exhausted with the hard, hard farm work, so did the soil in the cultivated fields. John observed that after four or five years of farming, the Fountain Lake farm soil became unproductive. For example, when they first began farming, they would produce twenty to twenty-five bushels of good wheat per acre. Now they were only getting five or six bushels per acre. Like Daniel, many of the immigrants from Europe didn't know how to farm. Gradually, like other new farmers learning to farm, Daniel discovered that English clover would grow even in the exhausted fields. He learned from other farmers that when the mature clover was ploughed under and then the field was planted with corn or wheat, amazingly, rich, hearty crops were harvested. Who knew that English clover could be such a wonderful natural fertilizer? Maybe Daniel was right when he said that God will provide. (48)

One morning after breakfast, Daniel announced to his family. "Well, my dear family, after eight years of hard work in making our beautiful Fountain Lake farm and getting it in perfect order, I bought a half-section of land about four or five miles to the eastward for our new farm. Yes, we'll start all over again! Isn't that wonderful news? God really does provide for us!"

John, like his siblings, and probably his mother as well, thought to himself, *"Yes, we'll have to clear and break up other fields for a new farm, then fence them in, which will only double all the work we've already done, such as heart-breaking tree chopping, stump-digging, fence-building, barn and house building, among many other things!"*

Being the oldest boy, now almost nineteen years old, John walked for two growing seasons from Fountain Lake to Hickory Hill to help cultivate it. Daniel also hired some other workers to help with it, but John bore the brunt of the heavier work. Daniel also hired carpenters to help him build a log house for temporary shelter for the family, and a stable for their animals. These would do until they could build a permanent house and a larger barn. The family moved to their new farm about the time of Sarah's marriage to David Galloway in December, 1856.

In 1857, Daniel, with the help of local carpenters, built a frame home. Located on a high slope, the family would have a panoramic view of the country side. The two-story house was in the shape of a T and had a cellar that could be reached by an outside entrance as well as from a trap door inside.

Daniel called their second farm 'Hickory Hill' because it had many hickory trees surrounding it. The land was better and richer than the Fountain Lake farm land, but there was no natural water source, such as springs, streams or natural lakes. Therefore, a well had to be dug.

One morning in the fall of 1856, Daniel, John, David, and Danny gathered at the home site to begin digging the well. A neighbor, William Duncan, was also there to give Daniel advice on how best to dig it. William was also from Scotland where he was employed as a stone mason and miner.

Following Mr. Duncan's advice, Daniel set the three boys digging a short distance from where the new house would be built. "Start digging, boys! We'll only need a space of about three feet in diameter." Daniel then measured three feet in diameter and drew a circle to outline it using a small mining pick.

"You go first, John!" Daniel said.

"Yes, Papa!" John replied, not knowing what to expect, except that a well had to be dug, and water had to flow from it.

As always, Natura hovered overhead to watch for any evil spirits who might want to harm John, and he also wanted to be sure John was not injured by any of the work.

John dug for about thirty minutes. He was able to dig down about a foot through the top soil without hitting any rocks of any size.

"Okay, David, your turn!" Daniel ordered.

"Yes, Papa!" David began digging. He dug for another foot, piling the dirt around the large hole.

"Danny boy! You can begin filling the wheel-barrow with the loose dirt and haul it to where we'll have our first cultivated field." Daniel pointed to the exact location.

After four or five hours of digging, with Daniel and Mr. Duncan watching and giving some encouragement to the boys, John took his turn at digging again. After digging out another foot, he reached the ten-foot level and began to hit what was thought to be just a thin rocky layer of sandstone. But it wasn't. The 'thin layer' became a thick, solid layer of hard, solid rock.

"Well, Johnny," Mr. Duncan said, "I declare that you've hit bedrock. You can't dig anymore with the pick and shovel. We'll just have to blast the rock out!"

"What do you mean, 'blast the rock out'?" Daniel asked, looking puzzled. He'd never done any blasting of any kind and only thought of the danger involved in handling explosives.

"Well, Daniel, don't you fret any!" Mr. Duncan said. "I've done a lot of blasting in the mines back in Scotland. I know how to do it, and do it safely. Let's quit for the day since we can't dig anymore. I'll gather the explosives from the hardware store in Kingston this afternoon and return in the morning. We'll just give it a try...I mean give it a blast! If that's alright with you, Daniel?" He looked at Daniel for an answer.

"Okay, I guess. I just don't know what else to do in order to dig a well."

The next morning, Mr. Duncan returned to the home site and well hole with Daniel and his three boys. Mr. Duncan climbed down into the ten-foot hole, taking with him a hand drill with which to drill holes into the rock, and several sticks of dynamite. He drilled five holes around the bottom perimeter of the well hole, placed a stick of dynamite in each hole, placed explosive wires with caps into each stick, and carried the lead wires with him as he climbed up a ladder out of the hole.

Hooking the wires to a hand-pump detonator, he instructed Daniel and the boys, "Now, Daniel, you and your boys go over behind the little barn you've built so you don't get struck with any rocks that might come flying out of the hole. I've got my hard hat on to protect me, and I've done this many times before. I should be alright!"

Daniel and the boys followed Mr. Duncan's instructions. Then Mr. Duncan shouted, "Fire in the hole! Fire in the hole!" He then raised the handle of the detonator and pushed it down as hard as he could.

"Kaboom! Kaboom! Boom! Boom! Boom!" In rapid succession went the explosions from the five sticks of dynamite.

Natura hovered over Daniel and the boys to protect them from any flying rock debris. Only a few pebbles flew in their direction. Very few even reached Mr. Duncan as close as he was.

Mr. Duncan ran to the hole. Daniel and the boys also ran to the hole. Looking into it, expecting to see much of the hard rock loosened, there was hardly any.

Looking a bit dumbfounded, Mr. Duncan said, "Well, men, we'll just have to do another blast. Sometimes it takes two or three blasts to loosen the rock enough!"

Mr. Duncan climbed down the ladder, drilled more holes, placed the sticks of dynamite in them, wired them, and climbed out of the hole. After connecting the wires to the detonator, he went through the same warning as before detonating the dynamite. Checking the hole once again, very little rock had been loosened. Mr. Duncan tried the blasting for a third time. Same result.

Now looking very disappointed, he said, "Daniel, looks like the blasting just isn't doing any good. Not sure what you should do now to dig your well. You could use a hammer and chisels but that'd take you a long, long time I think."

"Well, Mr. Duncan, thank you for trying to blast the rock. I guess we have no other choice but to hammer and chisel the rock out. We've got to have a fresh water well because we have no other means of getting drinking water."

Daniel decided that the best way to dig it was to use a mason's chisel along with a hammer to dig it out. Poor John was chosen to be the one to dig it.

"Well, John, since you're the oldest and strongest, you'd better start this afternoon hammering and chiseling that rock."

"Yes, Papa!"

"And you, David and Danny, you can help John. We'll hook up a bucket with a rope under a well frame for John to place the rock in, and you two can pull up the bucket to empty it."

"Yes, Papa!" David and Danny said about the same time.

Mr. Duncan helped Daniel and the boys build a well rig with a handle, tied a long rope around the handle bar, tied one end of the rope to the bucket, and lowered the bucket into the ten-foot-deep hole. John climbed down the ladder to the bottom of the hole with a mason chisel and a large hammer to begin chiseling at the hard rock. Chipping away at it, he began to make some progress, placed the loose rock pieces into the bucket, and told David and Danny to pull up the bucket to empty the rocks. Day after day, John, David, and Danny worked at digging the well through the hard rock. When the well got too deep to use a ladder, Daniel and the two boys would lower John down into the hole as he sat on the bucket with both legs crossed around the bucket to hold himself steady.

Daniel and the boys would go away to work in the fields. They would return at lunch time to hoist John out, let him eat lunch, and then return him to the hole once again. John would work in the hole, chipping away at the rock until night. Natura hovered around John to keep him safe, making sure John didn't slip off the bucket and fall into the well. This work went on from morning until dark, day after day, week after week, and eventually month after month.

One morning when the well was eighty feet deep, John was lowered into the well as usual. He normally filled the bucket with the chips from the day before and Daniel and the boys hauled the bucket up to empty it. But because of deadly choke-damp, a carbonic acid gas, had settled at the bottom of the well during the night, John began to lose consciousness. He swayed back and forth on the bucket because of the poisonous gas.

Daniel became alarmed that John did not make any sounds. "What's going on John? Why aren't you filling the bucket with the rock chips?"

John did not reply.

As John was leaning against the side of the wall, Natura began to blow the poison gas upward to clear it away from John. Serpenta, on the other hand, blew the gas back toward John. It became a battle of which spirit could blow the hardest and sustain it. John, of course, was caught in the middle, gasping for fresh air. Natura knew he needed help. He stopped blowing long enough to focus his energy in a message to his friend, Guardian Angel Harry, who immediately heard Natura's urgent request. Harry instantly rushed to the well hole, entered it, and stood next to Natura.

"Thanks for coming so quickly, Harry!"

"You're welcome, Natura. I can see that our evil spirited Serpenta is up to no good as usual. We'll both blow the poisonous gas away from John and overpower Serpenta's ability to blow it back. If we're lucky, we'll also blow Serpenta up the well and out into eternity. Ready, set, blow!"

As Natura and Harry blew together, a hurricane force of air blew all of the poisonous gas away from John and out the top of the well. The force caught Serpenta with such great pressure that he was also was blown out of the well.

After a blast of air mysteriously blew out of the well, Daniel could now see John, barely hanging onto the bucket, although Natura was holding him up, keeping him on the bucket. Turning toward Harry, Natura said, "Thanks my good friend. I couldn't have done it without you!"

"You're very welcome Natura. I'll be going now. I believe you can take care of John without my help, now that Serpenta is out of your way." Harry disappeared and returned to his home base with Archangel Michael and his army of spiritual warriors.

"Help, Papa, please get me out!" John could barely talk.

Shouting now to John, Daniel said, "Get into the bucket! Hold onto it very tightly!"

With Natura's help, by pushing and supporting John, he managed to stay on the bucket. Daniel and David pulled with all their strength to haul John up out of the well. Afterward John could only remember that he was dragged out, and that he was trying to breathe in fresh air.

The next day, Mr. Duncan heard about the near fatal accident with the deadly choke-damp gas. He came to see Daniel and John to hear more about the event details.

Afterward he said to John, "Well, it's only by God's good mercy that you're still alive. Many of my friends I worked with in the mines are now dead because of choke-damp poisoning. But I've never heard of any escaping it like you did!"

When Natura heard Mr. Duncan say this, he beamed with angelic pride that he along with his friend, Harry, had saved John's life.

Mr. Duncan instructed Daniel how to throw water down the hole to help absorb the gas. He also told Daniel to attach a bundle of brush to a light rope and drop it again and again in order to carry down pure air down into the hole, and to stir up the poison.

After only a day, when John had recovered from the shock, Daniel lowered him again to the bottom of the well, but only after taking the precaution stir it up well with a brush bundle and to test the air with a lit candle.

John continued with his hammer and chisel chipping as before until he was ninety feet down. At last John struck pure water that gushed up to begin filling the deep well. After Daniel and the boys pulled John out with the bucket, they built a covered top over the well, attached two buckets to ropes, and began drinking the purest of water for many years to come. (49)

# CHAPTER 19

## Corduroying Roads, Making New Friends

*"Corduroying the swamps formed the principal part of road-making among the early settlers for many a day. At these annual road-making gatherings opportunity was offered for discussion of the news, politics, religion, war, the state of the crops, comparative advantages of the new country over the old and so forth, but the principal opportunities, recurring every week, were the hours after Sunday church services." John Muir (50)*

After Wisconsin became a state in 1848, counties and towns began to provide public services for its citizens. One of those services was to build public roads. Marquette County divided the county into road districts and its citizens were responsible for building the roads for their district. Road building by the citizens became an annual event for them to gather, build roads, and, of course, to socialize. Road building across the marshlands was particularly difficult. The builders had to lay tamarack tree logs in crisscross fashion over the marshland and then fill the spaces between the logs with brush and dirt. Tamarack trees, straight and tall, were commonly found in nearby woods and seemed to be ideal for this use. (51)

In district six, Daniel was responsible for organizing the road building. He assigned John to work with his young neighbors, Davie Taylor and Davie Gray, in the building of a corduroy section of road from the pioneer cemetery, down the slope, and across the marsh toward the southern end of the county.

The three young men were a lot alike. They lived on farms near each other, shared similar lifestyles, enjoyed the boundless natural environment, and knew the same people. Each had similar desires as they searched for their purpose in life. And each had a wonderful talent for expressing themselves through the spoken and the written word. John and Davie Taylor had an added bond, both were keenly aware of the natural beauty around them. (52)

One day in 1855, the three boys met at the pioneer cemetery to begin their work project. (53) "Well, good morning Davie and Davie," John said. "It sounds like I'm repeating myself when I meet up with you fellows together. What part of the work do you two want to do?"

Both Davies knew that John was the best tree cutter and wood chopper in the county, so it was easy for them to suggest he do the tree-cutting.

"Funny that you ask, John," Davie Taylor replied. "We know how well you cut trees and trim them. Everybody in the whole county knows. So, why don't you do that part of the work and we'll lay the logs down onto the marshland. We can then work together to fill the spaces with brush and dirt."

"Sounds like a good plan," Davie Gray said.

"That's fine with me, fellows," John replied. "I brought two of my sharpest and best axes just for that purpose."

John walked ahead of the two Davies to the nearest tamarack tree, placed his axe at the base of the tall tree, and swung with a few well-aimed and hard strokes. Down the tree went! John quickly trimmed the limbs from the tree.

Natura watched John very closely as John swung his sharp axe. He knew how easily an accident could happen, either from the falling tree landing on John or John's axe glancing off a tree limb and striking him in his legs or feet.

"Okay, two Davies. Here's your first log to lay!"

"Wow!" Both Davies said at the same time. "You really mean business, Johnny Muir!"

"Never seen anything like that in my life!" Davie Taylor said as he picked up one end of the long log and Davie Gray pick up the other end.

After John had cut and trimmed a half-dozen logs, the two Davies laid them in a crisscross fashion over the marshland. John stopped cutting down trees for a bit so he could help his two friends fill in the spaces with brush and dirt.

"We can fill my wagon with brush and dirt from the ridge near the pioneer cemetery. Then I'll lead Nob and Nell to pull the wagon near the logs to unload it." John announced.

"Thanks for your offer, John," Davie Taylor replied. "That'll help us a lot to get this project completed."

"Even with the aid of your wagon and horses," Davie Gray said, "it'll take us a few weeks to lay enough logs, fill the spaces, and completely build a corduroyed road."

When the three boys stopped to eat lunch each day, they enjoyed talking about poetry they'd read. They often recited some lines from their favorite poets. Being devoted to the Scottish poet, Robert Burns, John had memorized many of his poems and could easily recite them. Mr. Burns was a Scottish poet and lyricist who was widely recognized as the national poet of Scotland. In later years, as John sauntered on his many walks in nature, he carried a copy of Burn's poetry book in his backpack to read to remind him of Scotland, and also his home. John also sang many of Burn's lyrics to keep himself company on his long, lonely walks. John and the two Davies also talked about the classic literature books they'd read. For example, the two Davies discussed and quoted Charles Dickens while they worked. (53) Mr. Dickens was one of the most famous writers of nineteenth-century England. His many books were filled with stories of poor English people struggling to simply make a living, and finding their own personal strengths to help them succeed.

"Oh, how wonderful to hear the stories written by Mr. Charles Dickens!" John said. "I'd love to read his books! I do believe I could read about his works and characters day and night!"

“Why John, you can read them!“ replied Davie Gray. “I have several of his books at home and will bring them to you tomorrow morning. You can borrow them for as long as you wish.“

“Yes, John, I too have a few classic literature books you may also borrow.“ Davie Taylor said.

Davie Gray’s imagination had been widened and inspired only a year ago when he met Davie Taylor who had a deep, spiritual-type love for poetry and literature. (54) Likewise, John was caught up in the flaming spirits of both boys. The exciting discussions, day after day, with the two Davies filled John with much delight. It inspired him to read and learn from books, something he had not done since his early schooling in Scotland.

John thought to himself as he went to sleep one night after a long, hard day of corduroying roads, and most especially after conversing with the two Davies about interesting poetry and literature, “*In the five or six years since coming to America, I’ve worked hard on the farm. I’ve taken no time to fill my hunger for learning. The few books that father has are mostly of a religious nature, such as the Bible. He believes strongly that the Bible is the only book we need to guide us. Somehow, I must find a way to gain more worldly knowledge.*”

The next morning, John and the two Davies met at the pioneer cemetery to continue their corduroy road building, and, of course, to continue their inspiring conversations about famous authors.

“Good morning to you, Davie and Davie!” John said as he jumped from his wagon. He excitedly ran to shake the hands of his friends.

“Good morning, John!” Davie Gray said while giving John a hardy handshake and a pat on his shoulder. “Top of the morning, John!” Davie Taylor said, rigorously shaking John’s hand, and handing him some books. “Here’re three of Charles Dickens’ book you can borrow as long as you like!” Taylor handed him copies of *David Copperfield, Oliver Twist, and Little Nell.*

“Great Scot, how thoughtful of you Davie!” John took the books and held them up high as if could worship them. “I’ll be reading all of these tonight for sure!”

John turned and placed the three books carefully on his wagon seat. He then grabbed two of his sharpest axes in preparation for cutting down and trimming lots of tamarack trees.

"I can see that you're ready to work, John!" Davie Gray said. "Let's get on with our work! Ready to go, Davie Taylor?"

"Ready as I'll ever be, Davie! But I'm not sure I'm ready to keep up with John Muir's splendid cutting and trimming!" John gave a humble smile to both Davies. The three young men kicked up their feet as if to start dancing, and then ran a short distance to begin their day's work.

Natura was hovering over John's head, as usual, to make sure he was not injured in any way. Natura also continued to be watchful for any signs of evil spirits lurking in the nearby woods, looking for an opportunity hurt John. He could never be too watchful for Serpenta who was intent on discouraging, embarrassing, or hurting John any way he could.

John had felled and trimmed two trees in a very short time. He took a few steps toward the next tree, a very tall one near the road where they were working. Looking up at the tall tree and carefully measuring where he wanted it to fall, he expected it to fall a few feet away from the roadway where the two Davies were working, filling in the log spaces with brush and dirt. John felt sure he was ready to begin the cut. He swung his axe well behind his muscular back and brought the axe forward to make a deep cut into the tree. Once again, looking at where he wanted the tree to fall, he swung again and again, making excellent deep cuts into the tree's large round base. Serpenta saw an opportunity to embarrass John by making the tree fall on the two Davies or very near them to scare them. As John made his final cut into the tree, Serpenta positioned himself near the tree's top and pushed his energy field into the tree causing it to fall toward the two Davies. Grinning crazily, he muttered, "*Ah, John's two Davies, once his friends but who knows after this tree falls on them!*"

Now seeing the tree falling toward the two Davies, John froze in disbelief! He could only think of warning his two friends of the danger of the tree slowly falling toward them! "Watch out Davies! That trees falling toward you! Get out of its way! Now!"

The two Davies heard John's warning, then looked up to see the tree coming down toward them! Natura also saw the tree falling and heard John's warning. He didn't want to see the two Davies hurt or killed nor did he want John embarrassed or feeling badly about his tree cutting misjudgment. Natura quickly flew to the tree, wrapped his huge wings around the top, and carried it in a direction away from the two Davies. They couldn't believe that now the tree was suddenly falling well away from them. John couldn't believe it either! Dropping his axe and running toward the two Davies, John greeted them with a hug of relief and sweet victory!

"Wow, John! Thought we were goners!" Davie Taylor said with his eyes big as melons.

"Me too, John! I prayed like I've never prayed before for God to save us!" Davie Gray breathed heavily as great relief shown on his young bearded face.

John was speechless! He managed to mutter, "Oh dear fellows, I'm so sorry! The tree didn't fall where I thought it would. It seemed like a strong wind caught it and pushed it toward you! How that happened, I don' know! Please forgive me! I'll be sure to fell other trees well away from you!"

"Please don't worry, John!" Davie Taylor said. "It wasn't your fault. We're lucky we're alright."

"Yes, John, not to worry!" Davie Gray said. "Our good Lord is watching over us. Believe me, prayers do work because He certainly heard my prayer."

Natura couldn't agree more with Davie Gray. He knew that through prayer and God's mercy, he'd received a spiritual message to push the tree safely away from the two Davies. All was well!

The three young men resumed their work and took greater care in doing it safely. It was hard work but very rewarding as the three friends enjoyed each other's company and shared their dreams for a happy future. The building of their corduroy road took about three weeks to complete. The day after they finished it, Daniel Muir gathered with the three young men and the entire community to dedicate it. He gave special thanks to John and the two Davies, and thanks to God for a straight and smooth road on which to travel. Daniel also encouraged the citizens to continue the road building so that everyone could enjoy their wonderful benefits.

# CHAPTER 20

## *Knowledge and Inventions*

*"I learned arithmetic in Scotland without understanding any of it, though I knew the rules by heart. But when I was about fifteen or sixteen years of age, I began to grow hungry for real knowledge, and persuaded father, who was willing enough to have me study, provided my farm work was kept up, to buy me a higher arithmetic book. Beginning at the beginning, in one summer I easily finished it without assistance, and in the short intervals between the end of dinner and the afternoon start for the harvest and hayfields, accomplishing more without a teacher in a few scraps of time than in years in school before my mind was ready for such work. Then in succession I took up algebra, geometry, and trigonometry and made some progress in each, and reviewed grammar." John Muir (55)*

John loved to read, but his father had brought only his Bible and a few religious books from Scotland. Fortunately, several of his neighbors, like the two Davies, had acquired all sorts of books. John borrowed as many as he could and read them at every opportunity he had. But he had to keep them hidden from his father. Among these borrowed books were several Scottish novels, which like all other non-religious novels, were forbidden by his father. Nevertheless, John read them with much eagerness, although in secret from his father.

John happily discovered that the Bible's poetry, and the writings of Shakespeare and Milton inspired him to no end. He became increasingly excited to know all the poets and classical literature authors. He saved up small amounts of money to buy as many of their books as possible. Within a few years he was very proud to own some books by Shakespeare, Milton, Cowper, Henry Kirke White, and Campbell. (56) However, there was little time for reading. He had only a few stolen minutes, now and then, between his field work and chores. One night as he was sitting in the living room with his father, John asked his father for permission for time to read. (57)

"If you must read, John, you may get up in the morning to do it. You may get up as early as you like."

"Thank you so much, Papa!" John was ever so grateful, for he knew this was difficult permission for his strict father to give him.

The first morning John got up at one o'clock! He was greatly overjoyed to have gained five hours for reading. John also was interested in inventing different things. He thought to himself, *"That's almost half a day!"* He hardly knew what to do with it!

He first thought of reading in the house but it was so cold that he'd have to have a fire to stay warm. *"What shall I do?"* he thought.

About that time, it seemed that the rug over the trap door to the cellar moved on its own. However, Natura knew what John was thinking and thought that the cellar's relatively warmer space would be tolerable for John to read and to work on his invention ideas. However, he'd need a candle to see in the dark cellar.

John decided to go to the cellar through the inside trap door. While John truly enjoyed reading, he also enjoyed inventing things and making models of them. *"Why not work on a model of a self-setting sawmill I've invented in my mind?"* John thought. He opened the trap door slowly so as not to wake anyone in the house, especially his father and mother whose bedroom was directly above the cellar space where he'd be. He lit a large candle and went down the stairs to the cellar. (58)

Natura followed closely behind. As always, Natura watched over John very closely. While John was working in the cellar, Natura warmed his angelic body and gently flapped his large wings to blow a little heat toward John.

John was truly filled with joy to be able to read in the cellar, but was more joyful to be able to work on his inventions! He only had a few tools with which to work: a vice, a few files, a hammer, and some chisels. Being the inventor that he was, he was able to make his own bradawls, punches, and a pair of compasses out of wire and old files. "*Now, what to do for a saw for cutting my wood?*" He thought. Looking around he found an old-fashioned corset containing a strip of steel that he formed into a fine-tooth saw. It was crude saw but it'd work to cut his wood.

Now with enough tools to work on his self-setting sawmill model, John began to cut out the many pieces from some scrap wood his father had given him. Sawing, whittling, and shaping his intricate pieces, John laid the pieces out on an old table. Soon he was putting pieces together just as he imagined in his head. All of this tedious wood work was done right under his father's bedroom!

The next morning John somehow got up at the same time, one o'clock. The temperature in the cellar was just a little below freezing. As before, John lit a candle to see enough to continue work on his little sawmill model. Natura warmed his invisible body and flapped his wings to help warm the cold cellar. Early morning after early morning, John went to the dark cellar to work on his model. Finally, one morning his father just had to say something about the early-morning time John was getting up.

"John, you've been getting up quite early every morning for the past week. It seems you're going down into the cellar to do something. I can hear you at times working with a saw, hammer, and other tools. Just what are you doing?" (59)

"Papa, I'm working on a self-setting sawmill model for improving the way logs are cut into lumber. I've had this idea in my head for a while and it just needs to be expressed."

"I see, John, but must you get up so early to do it?"

"Remember, father, you gave me permission to get up as early as I wanted."

"Yes, I did indeed! Why I did that I don't know. But I did and I won't take the permission back. But could you be a little quieter when you're working down there?"

"Yes, Papa, I'll try. And thank you again for allowing me the time to do my work."

After John completed his self-setting sawmill, he took his model and dammed one of the streams in the meadow. He then put the little sawmill into operation. How well it worked! John followed this invention making many others, all from scrap metal and wood. These inventions included waterwheels, curious door locks and latches, thermometers, hygrometers, pyrometers, clocks, a barometer, an automatic contrivance for feeding the horses at any required hour, a lamp-lighter and firelighter, and an early or late rising machine. John also learned the time-keeping principles, using the pendulum, from one of the books he'd borrowed. So, he made plans to build one. Using scraps of wood, he whittled the very detailed clock parts, put them together, and built a wonderful pendulum clock. (60) He finished it and placed it in the house parlor for all the family to enjoy.

John found it impossible to stop inventing and whittling. The passion was deep down within him and needed to be expressed. He began working at his inventions faster and faster, it seems. He also made a hickory clock, shaped like a scythe to symbolize the scythe of Father Time. For the pendulum, he used a bunch of arrows that he thought symbolized 'the flight of time'. John hung the finished clock on an oak snag that seemed to show the effect of the passing of time. On the handle of the scythe, John wrote these words: 'All flesh is grass.' John got this phrase from the New Testament book of I Peter 1:23-25 which reads, "You have been born anew, not from perishable but from imperishable seed, through the living and abiding word of God, for: 'All flesh is like grass, and all its glory like the flower of the fields; the grass withers, and the flower wilts; but the word of the Lord remains forever.'" This Biblical inscription pleased John's father. In addition, the whole family liked it and admired John for building it. (61)

John was growing restless. Although he was learning and inventing, he felt the need to spread his wings, like one of his favorite birds, and simply fly away. His brothers, David and Dan, had already left the farm when they were of age. John sorely missed their company and often wondered how they were doing. Nevertheless, John stayed a year longer on the farm, but deep inside he really wanted to leave home.

Natura sensed this restlessness in John and wanted to help. But what could he do?

John continued to wonder what would he be in life. John's mother hoped he might be a minister. His sisters thought he'd be great inventor since he had invented and made so many wonderful things. But John sometimes thought he'd like to be a physician, but he didn't have the money for such a long-term education. Given his knack for tools, machines, and inventive ideas, John decided he should work in a big machine shop or factory. At this time in his life, that's all he knew how to do well. As a matter of fact, he was considered to be a genius at doing it. (62)

Only God and, of course Natura, knew what John was to do in life. He was to be a sort of guardian angel to remind people to protect and care for the world's natural things. Without people like John to write and preach about conserving God's natural things, greedy people would soon overuse them. However, he also knew that John needed to experience other things in life before his true purpose in life was revealed to him. Natura's job was to protect John and to guide him with gentle nudging whenever he could.

One day, John started talking about his career plans with Mr. William Duncan, a Scottish neighbor, who was very interested in John's welfare. Mr. Duncan took time to give John a listening ear and also to encourage him.

"John, if you really want to get into a machine shop or a factory, just take some of your wonderful inventions to the State Fair in Madison. I'm sure that as soon as the judges, and perhaps some manufacturer, sees what you've made, they'll be happy to open their doors to you. Why, any shop in the country would love to have you! You will surely be welcomed everywhere!" (63)

John was so encouraged by Mr. Duncan that he made up his mind to leave home. He decided he would take a chance and go to the State Fair in Madison.

# CHAPTER 21

## *Inventions at the State Fair*

*"The aching parting from mother and my sisters was, of course, hard to bear. Father let David drive me down to Pardeeville, a place I had never before seen, though it was only nine miles south of the Hickory Hill home. When we arrived at the village tavern, it seemed deserted. Not a single person was in sight. I set my clock baggage on the rickety platform. David said goodbye and started for home, leaving me alone in the world. The grinding noise made by the wagon in turning short brought out the landlord, and the first thing that caught his eye was my strange bundle. Then he looked at me and said, 'Hello, young man, what's this?" John Muir. (64)*

John stayed overnight in Pardeeville, finding room at a little tavern, where he waited for the train for Madison to come the next day. The next morning, he went to the train station to purchase his ticket for Madison. Soon a great locomotive, the first John had seen in America, came into the station.

John marveled at the giant locomotive as it slowly came to a stop. It seemed like its wheels were as tall as he was! He wondered how such a large machine could even pull its own weight much less the many cars connected to it. The steam from its inner workings excitedly raced through the air carrying its energetic sounds with it.

A few passengers stepped off the passenger car and were greeted by either family or friends. The conductor stood at the bottom of the steps to help each passenger step down. And then it was time for the Pardeeville passengers to board the great train.

John took his bundle of inventions to the conductor before he could board the train. (66) "Hello, young man! You'll need to take your bundle of things to the baggage car to check them. They'll be safer there and will be less likely to get broken."

"Yes, sir!" John walked along the side of the train until he found the baggage car where he checked his bundle to Madison.

With much excitement, John raced back to the conductor. "Sir, I wonder if I can ride on the locomotive engine?"

Seeing the excitement on John's face, the conductor replied, "I don't see why not, young man. Go up there and check with the engineer first. I'm sure there'll be no problem with you riding up there with him."

John went to the engineer to ask him about riding on the engine. "Hello, sir, the conductor said to ask you about riding on the engine to Madison. He thought it'd be alright."

"I don't care what the conductor told you, or what he thinks! I've got my own orders to obey, and you can't ride on the engine!"

John returned to the conductor to tell him about the engineer's answer. "Well, young man just come with me and I'll talk with the engineer. I'm sure that after he knows more about you, he'll let you ride on the engine."

Sure enough, after the conductor explained to the engineer the nature of John's inventions and his interest in machines, the engineer allowed John to board the engine. Once the train left the Pardeeville station, John got permission from the engineer to walk along the foot-board to the front of the engine where he seated himself on the cow-catcher.

To ensure that John didn't fall off the train, Natura hovered beside him, keeping pressure on John's body to steady him. Once John had seated himself on the cow-catcher, Natura wrapped one of his large wings around John's body, sort of like a seat belt, to hold him securely to the train.

What a wild and thrilling ride for John! He felt like he was literally flying through the air and his body was being pushed through the scenic landscape as if in a wonderful dream!

Arriving in Madison around noon, John jumped from the train and graciously thanked the engineer and the conductor for the wonderful ride. He grabbed his bundle of inventions from the baggage car, walked to the ticket agent's window, and asked for directions to the fair grounds.

John followed the ticket agent's directions and walked toward the fair grounds. When he applied at the fair gate for admission, he was freely admitted and directed to the Fine Arts Hall. It was a very welcoming time for John. He was gladly given a place to display his inventions. The fair director was even so generous as to have a shelf built for John, along with placing John's name and that of his inventions on it. John quickly set up his clocks and his thermometer on the shelf. He placed his early-rising machine on the ground. After locating and placing the right size stones in his clocks, he had them running within twenty minutes. (65)

John's inventions instantly became a main attraction and many people arrived to praise John for his inventive work! "Why, young man, did you make these yourself?" a well-dressed lady asked John as she adjusted her spectacles, bent over to look at his clocks much closer, and then peered up at John.

John wore his home-made clothes which appeared worn and wrinkled, although fairly clean. His rather long hair was still tangled from the windy train ride and his beard was just beginning to cover his young face. He certainly looked like a country boy that he was.

"Yes, mam, I did!"

"Your clocks seem to work very well. Seems like you did a very good job following the plans when you put them together."

"Thank you, mam. The plans were in my head and I made each part by cutting and whittling pieces of scrap wood."

The lady's eyebrows raised. She slowly adjusted her spectacles to look at the clocks more closely, and then looked again at John, particularly at his appearance. "Well, young man, if you say so." She just couldn't believe that John had designed and made the clocks himself.

By that time, other people had arrived to view John's inventions. Soon the space in front of John's exhibit grew very crowded with people very eager to see his unique inventions. Many people asked John questions how he'd made the clocks and thermometer. John answered each person honestly and humbly. Most everyone present was truly amazed at John's inventions, and praised him highly as they moved on to see other exhibits.

The well-dressed lady seemed to believe that John, indeed, did make the inventions himself. However, she wondered how a young country boy could be so talented. She turned to leave. "Well done, young man. You certainly have a natural talent. I'm sure you have a good future of inventions ahead of you. Good luck to you!"

"Thank you, mam."

John appreciated the compliments from people but remembered the lectures from his father to avoid praise among all things. Natura observed all the happenings and was very proud that John's inventions were being highly regarded. However, he knew that John's ultimate purpose in life was to become a great naturalist who would remind people to preserve God's wonderful natural things. Natura also continued to watch-over John to protect him from any antics that Serpenta might introduce during the fair.

John also demonstrated his early-rising machine with the help of two small boys. He first explained how the machine would operate. As the two boys volunteered to lay down on the bed, John set the clock in motion to operate the bed. Within a few minutes, the bed reared up at a forty-five- degree angle and dispensed the boys onto the floor. The astonished boys greatly amused the crowds and everyone roared with laughter. Afterward, John demonstrated his washboard thermometer which was so sensitive it registered the changes in temperatures as people approached it, and then returned to its original position. (66)

The local newspaper reporters were also very interested as they made their rounds through the large hall. Following their visit, the reporters wrote quite good articles about John and his inventions with statements such as, *"How could a plain farm boy from rural Marquette County have invented and made such unique things?"*

When the prizes were awarded, John won a prize of fifteen dollars. He was so happy and truly overjoyed! What's next he thought? Natura knew what was next but he patiently waited for John to figure it out for himself.

While in Madison, John looked around to find out what else he could do to start his lifetime of inventions and get a job in a machine shop or factory. He happened to meet another inventor at the fair, named Norman Wiard. Mr. Wiard was exhibiting an iceboat he invented to run on the upper Mississippi River from Prairie du Chien to St. Paul during the winter months.

"Hello, young man, my name is Norman Wiard. That's my iceboat invention over there." Mr. Wiard pointed to the large iceboat exhibit across the large hall.

"Hello, Mr. Wiard. I'm John Muir, the inventor of these things you see here, plus a few more I left back home Marquette County."

John explained his inventions to Mr. Wiard and how he'd made them from plans in his head, using scraps of wood.

"That's truly amazing, John! You certainly have an inventive talent!"

"Thank you, Mr. Wiard. I'm hoping someone will see them and offer me some kind of job in a machine shop or factory."

"Well, John, I can't offer you a job until I see if my iceboat works successfully. But I can offer you some training. You can work with me in my foundry and machine shop in Prairie du Chien. I'll give you lessons in mechanical drawing and the use of mechanical books. Then, I'll show you what I do and then teach you how to invent things, build them, and use them."

John didn't think about Mr. Wiard's offer for very long. "Why, thank you very much Mr. Wiard. I accept your offer!" (67)

With that agreement, John gathered and bundled his inventions. He followed Mr. Wiard to his iceboat exhibit to help him load it. Soon, the large iceboat was mounted on a flat railroad car and John climbed aboard to travel to Prairie du Chien. Natura hovered close to John and watched over him on the long train ride from

Madison to Prairie du Chien, located on the Mississippi River in the western part of Wisconsin, just across from the State of Iowa.

John found a nice boarding house in Prairie du Chien where he could work for his board. He could also devote his spare hours to mechanical drawing, geometry and physics, along with learning how to apply these to machine building. However, John soon found out that Mr. Wiard was seldom at home. He thought that he was not likely to learn much by staying at Mr. Wiard's small shop. So, he decided to return to Madison where he earnestly hoped to enter the State University and get a good education.

# CHAPTER 22

## A State University Student

*"In Latin, I found that one of the books in use I had already studied in Scotland. So, after an interruption of a dozen years, I began my Latin over again where I had left off; and, strange to say, most of it came back to me, especially the grammar which I had committed to memory at the Dunbar Grammar School. During the four years that I was in the University, I earned enough in the harvest fields during the long summer vacations to carry me through the balance of each year, working very hard, cutting with a cradle four acres of wheat a day, and helping to put it in the shock. But, having to buy books and paying, I think, thirty-two dollars a year for instruction, and occasionally buying acids and retorts, glass tubing, bell glasses, flaks, etc., I had to cut down expenses for board now and then to half a dollar a week." John Muir (68)*

After John and Natura returned to Madison, February 1861, John earned a few dollars by making and selling a few of his early-rising beds that put sleepers on their feet each morning. He also made a few dollars addressing circulars in an insurance office. In addition, he paid for his board by taking care of a pair of horses and running errands.

But John wasn't satisfied with just earning his board. His great ambition was to enter the State University. So much that he wanted to do this that he just walked about the university grounds as often as he could. Indeed, he was charmed with its fine buildings, beautiful lawns, and many trees along the large Fourth Lake.

As he saw students going and coming with their books, he simply dreamed of becoming one of them. He thought that if he could only join them it would be the greatest joy of his life! He was desperately hungry and thirsty for knowledge, and was willing to endure anything to get it.

One day John met a student who had noticed his inventions at the Fair and recognized him. (69) "Hello there! Aren't you the inventor who had such wonderful things at the State Fair?" The student inquired.

"Why yes, I am," John replied, still a little shy of talking to just anyone on the street.

"What great inventions you had there!"

"Why, thank you, but I'd give anything to be going to this school you attend!"

Introducing themselves to each other, the student said, "Oh, very little money is required. You should be able to enter the freshman class with no problem given your talent for inventing things. And you can board yourself for around a dollar a week. Many of us do that and we live on bread, crackers, molasses, and milk. There's a baker and a milkman that come by the dormitory every day. You don't even have to go out shopping to buy it."

"Thank you, that's very encouraging. I think I'll just have to give it a try." With that encouragement, John called on Professor Sterling, the Dean of Faculty and acting President. (70)

Knocking on Professor Sterling's door one day, John heard the professor say, "The door is open; just come on it!"

Professor Stirling held out his hand and greeted John. "Hello, young man, I'm Professor Sterling. Welcome to the Wisconsin State University. What's your name and how can I help you?"

"Hello, Professor, I'm John Muir from Marquette County. I've been in Madison for my first time to show my inventions at the State Fair."

"Well, young man, please tell me about your inventions."

John then unwrapped his bundle of inventions to show to the professor. He was nervous as he explained how he'd made them. Then he demonstrated how each invention worked. Seeing that John was a bit disorganized, and of course nervous, Natura helped John by gently pressing on his hands to help direct him. When John finished his demonstrations, he breathed a great sigh of relief! And so did Natura!

"How remarkable, John! You've got quite an inventive head on you. So, what do you plan to do with your inventions?"

"I don't know. I just have these ideas and plans in my head. It seems like they just come to me and I have to somehow make them with my own hands. But what I want to do more than anything is to go to this university. I'd be the happiest person in the world if I could!"

"John, please tell me more about your education, training, and experience."

John told the professor about his education in Scotland, what he'd studied, and how well he remembered it. He also told him how he'd studied by himself at home to learn algebra, geometry, and trigonometry. John explained to the professor his love for poetry and classical literature, even to the point of reciting some poems and quoting some phrases from several authors.

At the beginning of the university's development, it was the school's policy to educate all Wisconsin students who wanted an education. The university's board and faculty understood that district schools, mostly rural at that time, did not fully prepare students for higher education. Many students just didn't have the necessary preparatory courses to enter, so the university was very lenient and flexible in admitting students.

Professor Sterling was very impressed with John. "Well, I tell you what, John Muir, I think you're just the kind of bright student this university is seeking to enroll. My answer to you is yes, yes, yes! Come join our students and faculty as soon as you can. We'd love to have you!"

Jumping from his chair, John did sort of a Scottish jig, and then literally shouted, "Professor Sterling, you've just made me the happiest person in the world! Thank you with all my heart!" John grasped the professor's right hand and shook it vigorously.

"You're very welcome, John! You'll be admitted to the university and will be placed in the preparatory department of the freshman class."

John thought he'd entered 'the Kingdom of Heaven'!

He didn't take the regular course of studies. Instead he selected courses he thought would be most useful to him, still thinking that he'd study to be a physician someday. In particular, he studied chemistry, mathematics, physics, botany, geology, and some Greek and Latin.

He received his first botany lesson from a student by the name of Milton Griswold who gave him a detailed lesson using the pea family as an example.

One day in June, John was standing on the steps of the north dormitory where he lived. Milton came up to him and began to teach. He reached up and pulled a flower from the overhanging locust tree, and handed it to John. (71)

"Muir, do you know the family name of this tree?"

"No, I don't know much at all about the field of botany."

"Well, what other flower does this locust flower remind you of?"

"A pea flower."

"You're absolutely right, Muir!"

John shook his head a bit wondering what Griswold just said.

"How can that be, Griswold, when the pea seems so weak and clings to a scrubby herb, while the locust flower belongs to a big hardwood tree?"

So, Griswold went on to explain that since their basic essential characters were alike, they somehow had to belong to the same family. Griswold went on to explain the similarities of the flower petals of both blooms as well as their leaves. After John had tasted the locust leaf, he discovered it tasted like a pea.

"Muir, you can't think that these similarities are just coincidences. I believe they show how the Creator who makes the pea vine and the locust tree had the same thought in mind when making them. Therefore, man just doesn't arbitrarily classify nature. In fact, man doesn't have anything to do with it. Nature takes care of it all by bringing amazing unity to its great variety. All that the botanist has to do is examine the plants to learn their relationships and how they are in harmony." (72)

That first botany lesson opened John's eyes, mind, and heart to the wonderful order of nature! It literally sent him running to the outdoors, into its woods and meadows, with wild, glorious expectations! Now his eyes were opened to nature's inner beauty, all revealing the magnificent designs of God's divine thoughts. It was truly a 'spiritual awakening' for John! From then on, he wandered into nature's inviting mystery every opportunity he had. He frequently made long hikes around Madison's lakes, gathering specimens, studying them, and classifying them. He kept his many specimens fresh in buckets of water in his room. After studying and learning his regular class lessons each night, he'd turn to studying his plant specimens.

John's room was filled with shelves containing glass tubes, jars, a variety of botanical and geological specimens, and a number of devices invented by John. One of these inventions was a curious-looking study table used by John to organize his book studying. Operated by a timing-device, also invented by John, the table placed John's textbooks in front of him to read for a specified period of time, moved the next book in place, and so on, until all books had been studied. John also made a machine to track the growth of plants relative to the action of the sunlight. (73)

Young Charles Vroman was John's roommate in his North Dormitory room. Charles was awed and amazed by John's many inventions. (74) After meeting John for the first time and looking around at the room, Charles said, "John, you have so many interesting inventions! How did you ever think them up and then make them?"

"Well, Charles, the images just naturally come into my brain. I don't know how. I just seem to see them in all of their detail. Then I begin sketching them out on a piece of paper. The next thing I do is find enough wood pieces to cut or whittle to look like the drawing. And finally, of course, I put them together and hope they work."

"It looks like they work alright, John!" Charles excitedly examined one device after another.

John's living arrangements at the University were very simple. He boarded himself in the dormitory and like many students, he provided his own food. Without enough money for a good daily diet of nourishing food, John mainly ate bread and molasses, graham mush, and sometimes a baked potato. He baked his potatoes on the hot ashes of the dormitory's wood furnace.

John studied very hard and quickly learned his lessons thoroughly. However, he was far from satisfied with what he'd learned, and thought about staying longer. But the dreadfulness of the Civil War continued to haunt him. During his stay at the university, the Civil War started and continued as long as he was there. Many of John's student friends volunteered to serve in the Union Army; many were also drafted to serve. So many students left the university that it was difficult to continue some classes. John personally learned about the war's horrors as some of his friends returned to Madison from battle, either dead or wounded. To John, this tragic war between the States appeared to have no end. It certainly didn't make sense to him that his newly adopted country with so many wonderful schools and churches was destroying itself from within by its own citizens. Although he would not necessarily dodge the draft if called, he was not particularly interested in waiting around to be called. John was also very restless and continued to be unsettled about what he'd do with his life. His brother, Dan, had already traveled to Canada to consider his purpose in life, which later turned out to be a medical doctor. John also thought that he wanted to be a doctor but knew he didn't have the money to attend medical school.

In the meantime, something deep inside him was being called to wander in God's beautiful world of pure nature. John knew in his heart and soul that this was his true calling, his true purpose in life. And so, he decided to leave the university and go on glorious botanical and geological excursions which lasted 50 years. While on that endless excursion, he was "always happy and free, poor and rich, without thought of a diploma or of making a name, urged on and on through endless, inspiring, Godful beauty". John left the university in 1863 for another, "the Wisconsin University for the University of the Wilderness". (75)

Only Natura and God knew what this meant for John. Natura, with his ability to see into John's future, knew the path that John would take. Leaving the University, John returned home after a brief excursion with two friends to the town of Prairie du Chien. He worked on the Muir farms for several months before deciding to travel to Canada. Leaving on a train March 1, 1864, John went on the first of his long wilderness excursions and botanized his way through Ontario, Canada, where he met up with his brother Dan near Niagara Falls, Canada. While Dan went on to medical school and became a doctor, John continued his wilderness excursions by returning to the United States. He later went on his famous 'thousand-mile walk' to the Gulf of Mexico (Cedar Keys, Florida). And then by a very unusual chain of events, he traveled to California where he wandered in the Yosemite Valley area, climbed its mountains, and studied how it was originally formed by glaciers.

He lived in California for the rest of his life where he continued his natural adventures of America's wilderness areas. Through many writings about his adventures, he shared his enthusiastic love for nature with the public. He beckoned people to come to the mountains and rest their souls. He also urged them to preserve America's natural lands for the enjoyment of everyone. John Muir influenced several U. S. Presidents and many Congressmen to create national parks to protect and preserve millions of acres of America's natural wilderness land. He directly influenced the establishment of the national parks of the Yosemite, the Sequoia, Mt. Rainier, and the Grand Canyon. And through his natural adventure travels to Alaska, he discovered Glacier Bay National Park. Therefore, it seems only right, and endearing, to call him 'the father of America's National Parks'.

The End

# SIGNIFICANT DATES IN JOHN MUIR'S LIFE

April 21, 1839-Born in Dunbar, Scotland, to Anne and Daniel Muir.

1849-The Muir family leave Scotland and move to Fountain Lake, Wisconsin, USA.

September, 1860-John Muir leaves home for the first time and takes his inventions to the Wisconsin State Agricultural Fair in Madison, Wisconsin. Afterward, John travels to Prairie du Chien with Norman Wiard, an inventor of an iceboat.

February, 1861-He returns to Madison and enrolls at Wisconsin State University, Madison, Wisconsin.

April, 1861-The American Civil War begins when Ft. Sumter in South Carolina was fired upon by rebel forces.

July, 1863-Leaves Wisconsin State University and travels by foot along the Wisconsin River to the Mississippi River. Returns to his home in Wisconsin and works on his brother-in-law's farm at Fountain Lake.

March, 1864-Leaves for Canada to join his brother Dan. Botanizes through Ontario as much as possible and then works at Trout's broom and rake handles sawmill.

March, 1866-After fire destroys Trout's sawmill, John travels to Indianapolis, Indiana, to take a job at Osgood & Smith carriage parts factory.

March, 1867-An accident to his eye temporarily blinds John causing him to leave factory work and pursue his deep interest in learning about nature.

September 1, 1867-After recuperation and regaining his eyesight, he begins a thousand-mile walk to the Gulf of Mexico ending at Cedar Keys, Florida (October 23, 1867).

January, 1868 to March 28, 1868-Travels to San Francisco and heads to Yosemite Valley for his first visit. Stays for ten years working, studying nature, and making scientific observations of glaciers in Yosemite Valley and the Sierra Nevada Mountain range.

1878-Writes mountain articles and submits them to Scribner's Monthly magazine.

1879-Makes first of seven trips to Alaska.

April 14, 1880-Marries Louie Strentzel, daughter of Dr. John and Louisiana Strentzel. Starts working on the Strentzel's large fruit ranch in Martinez, California.

March 24, 1881-Birth of first daughter, Annie Wanda Muir.

May, 1881-He travels to Alaska and the Arctic on the ship Corwin.

1882 to 1887-Spends much of his time working on the Strentzel's fruit ranch and being with his family.

1885-John's father, Daniel Muir, dies.

January 23, 1886-Birth of second daughter, Helen Lillian Muir.

1888-His wife, Louie encourages him to return to his writing and wilderness adventures.

1889-Writes two articles for the Century Magazine advocating that lands surrounding Yosemite Valley be made into a national park.1890

1890-The U. S. Congress approves a Bill to establish the National Park system. Sequoia National Park is established.

1891-John's sister Margaret and her husband, John Reid, move to California allowing John more time to venture into the wilderness.

1892-John is instrumental in founding the Sierra Club and serves as its president until his death. Yosemite National Park is established. Forest reserves are established in three states.

1892-David Muir, John's brother, moves to California and takes charge of the ranch management duties allowing John more time for writing and traveling.

1893-On a long European journey, visits Dunbar, Scotland, his boyhood home.

1894-His first book, Mountains of California, is published.

1896-His mother, Anne Muir, dies. John receives an honorary MA degree from Harvard University.

1897-Receives an honorary Doctor of Laws Degree from the University of Wisconsin.

1899-His sister, Sarah, moves to California.

1901-His second book, Our National Parks, is published.

1903-His sister, Annie Muir, dies in Portage, Wisconsin. She's the last of the Muir family living in Wisconsin.

1903-Camps with President Teddy Roosevelt in Yosemite and encourages him to protect western lands and forests from being destroyed. First federal wildlife reserve established.

1905-California recedes Yosemite Valley to the federal government for management.

August 6, 1905-John's wife, Louie Muir, dies.

1906-Sierra Valley National Park and Petrified Forest National Monument are established.

1908-Muir Woods National Monument is established.

1911-Pubishes his third book, My First Summer in the Sierra. Leaves on an extensive expedition to South America.

1912-Publishes his fourth book, The Yosemite.

1913-Publishes his fifth book, The Story of My Boyhood and Youth.

December 24, 1914-While visiting his daughter Helen in Daggert, California, John Muir catches pneumonia and later dies at a hospital in Los Angeles.

1915-Travels to Alaska published.

1916-A Thousand Mile Walk to the Gulf is published.

1917-The Cruise of the Corwin is published.

1918-Steep Trails is published.

1924-The Life and Letters of John Muir is published.

1938-John of Mountains: The Unpublished Journals is published.

# BIBLIOGRAPHY WITH FOOTNOTE REFERENCES

Front Book Cover: Nature's Prophet sculpture by Will Pettee, WJP Studios, 700 Cannery Row, Ste MM, Monterey, CA, info@wjpstudios.com, telephone: 831-717-4205.

Lorna Byrne, Angels in My Hair, Three Rivers Press, New York, 2011.

Chapter 1, footnote 1, p. 13

John Muir-The Eight Wilderness Discover Books, Introduction by Terry Gifford, Diadem Books, London; The Mountaineers, Seattle; 1992 (The Story of My Boyhood and Youth; A Thousand Mile Walk to the Gulf; My First Summer in the Sierra; The Mountains of California; Our National Parks; The Yosemite; Travels in Alaska; and Steep Trails).

Chapter 2, footnote 2, p. 724

Chapter 5, footnote 3, p. 27; footnote 7, p. 27; footnote 9, p. 27

Chapter 6, footnote 11, p. 36

Chapter 7, footnote 12, p. 35-36; footnote 13, p. 37

Chapter 8, footnote 15, p. 32; footnote 16, p. 39; footnote 17, p. 320-322; footnote 19, p. 33

Chapter 9, footnote 20, pp. 39-40; footnote 26, p. 40

Chapter 10, footnote 27, p. 42; footnote 28, p. 41; footnote 29, p. 42; footnote 30, p. 42

Chapter 11, footnote 31, p. 45

Chapter 12, footnote 32, p. 45; footnote 33, p. 45; footnote 34, p. 55; footnote 35, p. 46

Chapter 13, footnote 36, p. 51-52

Chapter 14, footnote 37, p. 77

Chapter 15, footnote 39, p. 56

Chapter 16, footnote 40, pp. 91-92; footnote 41, p. 91

Chapter 17, footnote 42, p. 61 & 63; footnote 43, p. 63; footnote 44, p. 60; footnote 45, p. 62; footnote 46, p. 64; footnote 47, p. 65

Chapter 18, footnote 48, pp. 94-95; footnote 49, p. 85; footnote 50, pp. 94-95

Chapter 19, footnote 51, p. 88

Chapter 20, footnote 57, p. 97; footnote 58, p. 99; footnote 59, p. 99; footnote 60, p. 99; footnote 61, p. 100, footnote 62, pp. 102-103; footnote 63, p. 102; footnote 64, p. 103; footnote 65, p. 103

Chapter 21, footnote 66, p. 104; footnote 67, p. 105; footnote 68, p. 106; footnote 70, p. 107

Chapter 22, footnote 71, p. 108; footnote 72, p. 107; footnote 73, p. 108; footnote 74, p. 109; footnote 75, p. 110; footnote 76, p. 110; footnote 78, p. 111.

Linnie Marsh Wolfe, Son of the Wilderness: The Life of John Muir, The University of Wisconsin Press, Madison, Wisconsin, 2003.

Chapter 5, footnote 4, p. 5; footnote 5, p. 10; footnote 6, p. 10; footnote 8, p. 13; footnote 10, p. 13

Chapter 7, footnote 14, pp. 3-4

Chapter 8, footnote 18, p. 16

Chapter 19, footnote 54, p. 40; footnote 56, p. 39

Chapter 20, footnote 61, p. 54

Chapter 21, footnote 69, p. 59; footnote 70, p. 61

Chapter 22, footnote 77, p. 66

Millie Stanley, The Heart of John Muir's World, Prairie Oak Press, Madison, Wisconsin, 1995.

Chapter 15, footnote 38, p. 8

Chapter 19, footnote 52, p. 15; footnote 53, p. 16; footnote 53, p 16; footnote 55, p. 15; footnote 56, p. 18

Roger Tory Peterson, Peterson Field Guides: Feeder Birds, Eastern North America, Houghton Mifflin Co., New York, 2000

Chapter 9, footnote 21, p. 38; footnote 22, pp. 23-29; footnote 23, pp. 23-29; footnote 24, pp. 78-79; footnote 25, pp. 50-51 & 78-79

www.ingramcontent.com/pod-product-compliance
Lightning Source LLC
Chambersburg PA
CBHW070359200726
48294CB00003B/986

* 9 7 8 1 9 6 0 9 3 9 2 9 6 *